The Bus Stopped

The Bus Stopped

Tabish Khair

PICADOR

First published 2004 by Picador
an imprint of Pan Macmillan Ltd
Pan Macmillan, 20 New Wharf Road, London N1 9RR
Basingstoke and Oxford
Associated companies throughout the world
www.panmacmillan.com

ISBN 0 330 41921 8

1 3 5 7 9 8 6 4 2

A CIP catalogue record for this book is available from
the British Library.

Typeset by Intype London Ltd
Printed and bound in Great Britain by
Mackays of Chatham plc, Chatham, Kent

for Adian

Acknowledgements are due to John Berger and Smriti Vohra for one purloined phrase each, to the editors of *Iron*, *London Magazine*, *The Source* (UK) and *StoryQuarterly* (USA) for accepting/publishing (slightly rewritten) sections from this book, and to Sam Humphreys, Aamer Hussein, Ide Hejlskov Larsen, Annette Lindegaard, Pankaj Mishra, Rebecca Senior, Peter Straus and Smriti Vohra, who first read the manuscript, for their advice, encouragement and support.

 Homes

More than the sahabs, bibis and babus, it was the servants who knew the lay of the two houses I grew up in, their scratched geography, their shadowed histories, their many voices of noon and curtaintude, evening and smokeliness. Because, more than the masters, it was the servants who had been midwives to the birth of the two houses that cradled our lives. Both the houses had grown up and wizened with them.

And yet, the two houses had also been painstakingly built by their masters: built not only with the material available but also with their dreams, hopes and eccentricities. Pillared with the breath of masters, mistresses, servants, the two houses had been home to us in childhood and early youth; for, as the adage goes, houses are built of brick but homes are made of breath.

I walk through one of the houses – the white one – with careful, muffled steps. The dust of my history lies heavily on this house. I do not wish to disturb these visible layers of accreted time. This is the house I will always know as Ammi ké yahan. At Ammi's place. Ammi's house. Though it was Ammi's husband, my grandfather, who built it. But Ammi – mother to my father and aunts, 'mother' to all her grandchildren (forcing our actual mothers to adopt more plastic designations – Amma, Mummy, etc.) – Ammi took over and reordered the house in the years when we were growing up, years in which her husband was first confined to a wheelchair by Ahlzheimer's and then, after a comatose state lasting seven years, buried in the family graveyard with genuine grief and genuine relief.

I skate across the other house's newly polished mosaic tile floor at the age of five or six. My shiny black school shoes slither and skid, and I imagine I am wearing roller skates. This house I have approached with a shout for many years. This house I still approach with something like a shout once a year. But the house no longer shouts back. Like an aged retainer, it smiles and grunts in reply. This house is the house of my parents. This house is simply house. Home. Ghar. There are times when I feel that this is the only home I have ever known, will ever know. No matter where I go, no matter how many years I stay away, this will be home.

Both sprawl in the compound bought by my grandfather, a compound approximately one kilometre long and half a kilometre broad. Opposite them, across the narrow Barrack Lines Road planted with rare tall teak trees, lie the barren brown fields and the marching barracks of the local police force. To the south and the east lie broken ranges of half-wooded hills. Only one of them has a history and a name that lingers – Brahmjoni, the womb of Brahma. To the north starts the town. A town named after a holy asura. Not a demon, an asura. For both the houses border the heart of a space that does not lend itself easily to translation. It is a space of many shades of skin, many dialects and languages spoken by servants and family members; a space of people, memories and practices that see no need to be called by another name. As jalebis are not just 'sweetmeats' and rotis and parathas are never just 'unleavened bread', an asura cannot be just a demon.

Ammi's house, the white one, was built by my grandfather – doctor, educationist and amateur archaeologist with some minor finds to his name. It was built during the Second World War, when cement was strictly rationed. As such, it was built not with cement but with a compound of lime and earth that, claimed my grandfather and the ancient master mason who supervised the construction, was the mix favoured by the Mughals for centuries before the hard certainties of cement and concrete. The area from which the soil was removed was turned into a large pond with grassy banks, into which my grandfather released zeera – of the delectable rehu fish. It lay behind the servants' quarters next to the white house, Ammi's house. The rest of the compound was developed into a landscaped garden, a tasteful combination of Mughal and Victorian elements, with a south end of fruit trees and a north end of the original wild growth, and a walk skirting the entire compound.

The white house had its particular relationship with servants. They lived in servants' quarters, an enclosed space constructed around a large courtyard and attached to the kitchen and the storeroom. Breakfasts and dinners were cooked in the kitchen and carried on large brass trays covered with thin cloth at least 200 metres into the drawing room. It was usual, Ammi would tell us later with a mixture of pride and complaint, it was usual to have at least ten guests eating at each mealtime. Breakfast, lunch or dinner. Invited guests, unannounced visitors, passing relatives, poor relations being educated by my grandfather, travellers from the ancestral village. People who would only eat with fork and knife and people who wouldn't care to touch them or know how to hold a fork, all eating together and as it suited them. Such a house craved its own quota of servants. It threw up servants – like the massive khansamah, Wazir Mian – who would never adjust to any other kind of house.

Not even to the house that my father built in the late sixties. My father's house, ghar to us, was just as massive a structure, built in the north end of the compound. Like his father, my father believed in continuity. It was built to resist the major earthquakes which hit the region once every fifty years or so. It stood, it stands, with the kind of beauty only silent strength can confer. It was built to defy time and house the next generation. It had a large dining table that could seat twelve people. All these things ought to have pleased Wazir Mian. But, alas, things had changed.

Ghar had only a three-room servants' quarters at the back. And even these were seldom used, most of the newer servants preferring to sleep in the verandas or one of the guestrooms. Its dining table would usually see only a guest or two during mealtimes. Wazir Mian was disappointed not in the house, but its accoutrements. Ghar required – and got – its own kind of servants. And the first sort could not always get along with the second.

But what about the servants themselves, you may ask. Didn't they have houses of their own?

Some did and many didn't. Some spent the years in Ammi's house or our house saving up to build a house and buy (or buy back) land in some distant village, to which they ultimately returned. Others did not bother, moving on from one house of service to another. But such was the distance between their houses and ours and so fleeting the occasions, such as a marriage, when we entered their houses that to tell of the houses of our servants would be impossible for me. We saw their houses only once or twice, if ever. They were in places where the bus stopped only for a minute, or not at all.

Journeys

1 ~

When he steps into the clearing it is not yet fully light. He walks to one of the buses parked in the clearing, an area which looks a bit like an abandoned field and a half-hearted attempt at starting a garage; he walks slowly, listlessly. There is no point getting worked up about another day, another dawn, though it is hardly a day or even a dawn yet, and the fat bastard would still be snoring on his cushioned khaat. There are tyres piled outside a corrugated shed. A crowbar lies half embedded in mud where he had dropped it a month ago and where it would lie until one day it caught the fat bastard's eye and gave him an apoplectic fit, serve him right, the mother-fucker. Some discarded motor parts are scattered around: a rusted mudguard, two or three handles, a cracked windscreen, small engine parts that he could name with his eyes closed. Tyres have worn deep grooves into the earth, though further down, near the barbed-wire fence, there is a stretch of irrigated and ploughed land where the fat bastard's wife, his own second cousin (on his mother's side), the once attractive Sunita, plants onions and garlic, cabbages and potatoes, all according to the season.

There are dewdrops on the windowpanes of the bus. Once in a while a drop quivers, hesitates and starts rolling down. Of its own volition or encouraged by the slight chilly breeze, it rolls, slowly at first, and then faster as it collects more drops, until it appears to be a narrow stream hurtling down, down, down, until it drops to the dirty earth.

He is a man who notices such things, he is a man who only notices such things; it seems to him, if he had noticed other things he would have been another man and not a bus driver plying one of the buses of his second cousin's husband. He sees life in still small images, almost frozen, and does not really know what image – momentous or incidental – would etch a particular moment or day or trip into his memory. Some people collect stamps or bottles or coins; he collects images, you have to collect something as worthless as images, don't you, no market value to them, and he has to collect them, nothing but them, images! images!, one from each trip of his life, thousands of them now, all meticulously remembered, just those single images, a colour, a scene, a face, an act italicized on the pages of memory. Not that he chooses the images consciously; that is simply the way his mind orders the seamless and yet unravelling days of his life.

He unlocks and opens the front door of the bus and a foul smell, the document of yesterday, is wafted away on the morning breeze. The man pulls himself up into the driver's seat, which is immediately illuminated by the yellow light that comes on. The passenger sections behind him are still dark, separated from his cubicle by rods that have been painted yellow to match the colour of the bus outside, with a narrower strip of brown and then a thin layer of bright red at the bottom of each rod – so that they almost look like pencils. Like a writer's pencil. Typical, he thinks, typical that everything should conspire to remind him of his failures, for once, before he dropped out of college, he had hoped to write novels, had even written fifty-seven pages of one in Hindi, that was long ago, long ago, and now he has to be penned in by these pencils that, like a writer's pencil, empower him – each trip a narrative made of the criss-crossing of other stories that board his bus and then go on unconcerned – even as they separate him from all that happens back there.

Over the dashboard is written this legend in Hindi, scrawled unevenly in what might have been scarlet lipstick, what *is* scarlet lipstick, he knows, for he still has that stubbed lipstick left behind by a whore with the huge metal nose ring, over the dashboard is scribbled: 'This place belongs to Driver Mangal Singh.' For a few seconds Mangal Singh sits there in silence, watching the dials and needles on his dashboard. They will come to life with the turn of the ignition key, needles quivering, dials lit up weakly. He fingers the metal whistle hanging around his neck. He looks at the house nearest to the bus, the three-storey home of the owner of the bus, the fat bastard, sleeping there, snoring with his arm around Sunita who had once been attractive and fun to be with; the house is lying still in the half-dusk, sleeping, breathing softly, the windows closed like eyelids. Just before he turns the ignition key, again and again coaxing the old engine to start, he puts the whistle to his mouth and gives a short sharp blow on it. A sound that cuts across the dawn, the field and the houses like a bird in flight.

2 –

I still remember the street urchins from the other day, their arms stretched rigid, index fingers pointing, mouths framing the word that I could hear loud as a gong even though they were out of hearing distance: hijra hijra hijra.

There was a time I could have been the keeper of the harem keys, a general, an adviser, a guard in the holiest of holy shrines – the . . . no, I will not name it in case some mullah takes offence. Those days eunuchs had a certain place in society, a role to play. In fact, a lot of this was because the prophet, peace-be-upon-him, considered us human beings – the third sex – and did not preach against us, though he discouraged castration even as a punishment. When Islam came to India, our position rose from that of untouchable curiosities to active and legitimate members of society. Before: we could not enter a temple, we could not adopt any profession except ritual dancing. After: we became advisers to young noblemen, artists, keepers of the harem keys, spies, soldiers, builders of cities, in one case even a famous general. That is why, in my ustad's house, we have always adopted Muslim names.

Even when we practised other faiths – because religion is
not such an issue with us as it is with men and women –
even then we adopted Muslim names. That is all, we were
told, the various generations of ustads in our house ever
asked of their chelas. That was our way of thanking the
religion that, for a short period, made it possible for us to
be ourselves.

All that, as you know, was long ago. Things changed,
middle-class morality or upper-caste religiosity – call it
what you will – struck back at us. Perhaps the coming of
the British, with their black and white theories, their
European values and their Victorian morality; the coming
of the British started our modern decline. You might be
surprised at me, a 'mere' eunuch, talking in such precise
terms, offering rational opinions. After all, you probably
associate us with those underdressed, overly made-up,
angular 'women' who jump at you on the streets and
demand money or who barge into marriage ceremonies
with loud songs and have to be paid to go away. That is
what we are now: that is what has happened to us. But
that is not what we were, or what we could have been.
We were trained to be dancers, artists, musicians, soldiers,
even scholars. We served, but we were seldom servants.
In some gharanas – my ustad ran one such – some vestiges
of self-respect and culture survived even into this century.
But it grew progressively harder to preserve such feelings
and attitudes in a society that increasingly shut its doors
on us. Once again, we were not part of society. We went

back to being curiosities and social untouchables, marginal
types, worse off than servants, something between a tart
and a circus freak. The age tried to break off our female
first names from our male surnames, for it is an age of
broken shards and jagged edges. Once again, we were
what other people thought we were and not what we
wished to be. And so, the old gharanas rotted and disappeared. Some turned into insulated and closed worlds,
others became dens of prostitution and petty extortion.
The gharana of my ustad simply fell apart after her death
and the death, soon afterwards, of the only man in the
household, her lover, the tabla player who was also our
music teacher. Some of us tried to run the gharana for a
couple of years, but our values and training were wrong.
We sought lovers, not customers. We wished to be given
gifts, not tips and hush money. Zohra Sheikh, the eldest
of us, drifted away, god knows where. One night her
wooden box lay under her charpoy and the next morning
both she and her box were gone. Razia, second in com-
mand, moved into another gharana within weeks of
Zohra's departure. This gharana was more in tune with
the times and Razia had always resented some of our old-
fashioned attitudes, had often berated Ustad for being out
of touch with the times. That left me and Chaand Baghi.
We had grown up together in the gharana and it was not
easy for us to leave. But within a few months it became
evident that we could not survive in the present state.
With the departure of Zohra and Razia, most of the

remaining patrons stopped coming too. It was not that we were unattractive. We were younger and more womanly than Zohra or Razia. But people just assumed that the gharana had dissolved. They stopped coming. Also, most of these patrons were old and they felt more at home with our elder sisters. So one day when Chaand turned to me and said, Farhana, I think I will go to my aunt in Bumbai, they say there are opportunities there – I simply replied, Whatever God wills, Chaand.

She touched me lightly on the cheek, hennaed fingers trailing down and then dropping away, but both of us knew that touching was no longer enough.

3 —

When Mangal Singh drives the bus, its yellow sides now glistening in the weak sun, into the stand behind the disused church and jumps out, only two of the five breakfast and tea stalls are open. But the first Gaya–Patna bus, a video express, is already revving its engine, its conductor calling out the fares, passengers hurrying into it or leaning on the barred windows sipping tea in earthen cups and glasses. The Patna–Gaya route has more and better buses than the Gaya–Phansa route that Mangal Singh plies. After all, Patna is the state capital. There are no video expresses on the Gaya–Phansa route, let alone buses like the non-stop tourist bus that sets off from outside Chanakya Hotel in Patna twice a day.

The two stalls had lighted their brick and earth ovens only half an hour back and their smoke still fills the stand with a soft haze. Some men wrapped in dark chaddars are sitting on the low benches outside the stalls; it sometimes seems to him that there are always men, perhaps the same men, who knows, sitting on the same short-legged benches. They are eating from pattals or chipped plates and sipping tea from squat, thick glasses. On one of the unoccupied benches he spots their new cleaning boy, Rameshwar: he is lying on the hard wood, precariously balanced, completely wrapped in a patched kambal of indistinct colour and design. He can tell it is Rameshwar, because that is where the boy sleeps every night. He pokes the boy with his index finger and tells him to get the bus cleaned. Wake up, son of a donkey, and wipe the mother-fucking bus clean with your arse, is what he actually says. The bundle starts stirring, mumbling and swearing. Come back for your breakfast, he adds, more kindly. He himself enters a stall and orders sabzi-puri.

A crow swoops down outside the stall.

4 −

Bearded, massive, uncompromising, Wazir Mian made life miserable for the long line of chokkra-assistants that he just had to have, and the longer sequence of cooks who followed in his footsteps and came up inevitably short.

There were things you had to know about Wazir Mian.

He had been the head cook of the Rajah of Mánpur, or some such colonial nobility, before he took over the reins of my grandfather's kitchen in the late forties. To ask him to cook just a family meal was to insult him. His recipes, my mother once said, must have been compounded only in terms of per dozen people. Not that he ever divulged his recipes. My mother and my aunts, no mean cooks themselves, spent many summer vacations trying in vain to identify that particular ground nut which added a delicate aroma to Wazir Mian's faluda and that particular spice which made Wazir Mian's murgh mussalam inimitable.

Wazir Mian guarded his culinary secrets with the same pride with which he guarded his reputation. After any elaborate dinner for guests, you had to call in Wazir Mian and congratulate him on the food. If you forgot to display him, he would consider it a criticism of the food and interrogate you to death. What was wrong, babu? Wasn't there a bit more salt in the korma? Do you think the kabab was underdone, and should have had a drop more papaya juice? If you finally replied that the food was good enough but you had simply forgotten to call him in after the dinner, Wazir Mian was capable of sulking for weeks. He once told me, in a perfectly matter-of-fact manner, that he would not deign to cook for a family that forgot such basic courtesy twice in one year.

For a long time, until I grew older and learnt to distinguish between them, I would tend to associate my first memory of Wazir Mian with the first painting or photograph I saw of Mount Everest. The two were always recalled together. One picture or presence always called up a faint memory of the other. It was an association that made sense at one level: Wazir Mian was a mountainous man. However, at another level, there was a discrepancy in the association. The picture of Mount Everest that I recalled was a kind of painting or a touched-up photograph depicting a prominently snow-capped peak. There was nothing snow-capped about Wazir Mian's head: he did not have many white hairs even in old age.

Older and mystified, I mentioned this to one of my aunts, and she reminded me of something I had forgotten. Evidently, in the early days, Wazir Mian did not just insist on being called in and congratulated after an elaborate dinner, he would come in wearing a proper chef's uniform. After all, he had been the chief chef of the Rajah of Mánpur. For Wazir Mian, this meant a flowing pathan suit with white overalls and the kind of tall chef's headdress – snow white and immaculately creased – that only five-star hotel cooks wear these days.

Evidently, Wazir Mian's mountainous presence was once capped with snow, but time and change had melted him down to black and greying hairs. The moral of the story was simple: even Wazir Mian was human.

5 -

Mangal Singh knows Shankar, the conductor, is furious with him. He could tell by the way Shankar banged his palms on the bus while calling out the fares, juntalman-Shankar with his pursed lips always at the maalik's pregnant purses, waiting for a drop to trickle out. But the maalik's purses have been getting more and more pregnant for seventeen years now and no delivery is eminent, no delivery at all, which is probably just as well for the world, it already has its quota of bastards and monsters.

He glances at Shankar pursing his lips. They have already been delayed by forty minutes, and Shankar blames him for the delay. He had met a couple of friends and, carried away by the gup-shup, he had spent more time over breakfast than he should have. Not that he cares.

And now they are well on their way. He is manoeuvring the bus through traffic thickening like curd on the narrow Phalgu bridge. The flanks of the bridge are rusted and you can see through them to the dry sand and the rivulets of dark water below. One has to drive carefully.

It is said that once the Phalgu had been a bubbly,

flowing river, going la-la-la on its own way like a virgin traipsing along the valleys, unaware of wolves and rapists. But it committed the sin of obstructing the path of the pregnant Sita, O Lord, O Lord. Or that Sita, carrying a child, had wanted to cross it (he does not really remember) and the Phalgu had refused to draw back and make a path for her when ordered, no respect for one's betters it showed, shitty communist virgin river. Sita had cursed it. May you turn barren, she had said. And bhadrdraam!

Now one has to wait for the monsoon or dig a metre into the Phalgu sand to find water. Most of the rivulets below have been dug out by dhobis and by their dhobins who, he knows from experience, have the most lascivious hips one could imagine, all that carrying of bundled-up clothes he guesses, and he gets an erection at the mere thought. Their washed clothes spread out on the sands, white, red, checks, stripes on the dull yellow of the cursed river. On both sides of the bridge, the Phalgu spreads its dotted, checked, striped yellow wings: a flattened and mounted butterfly of some extinct species.

6

I could smell Zeenat round the corner of the corridor. But then I was sixteen and exceptionally sensitive to the smell of women.

Women have different smells. I had always known that. The starched sari smell of my grandmother, the eau-de-cologne fragrance of my aunts, the talcum-and-attar scent of poorer relatives, the soap-and-sweat smell of the older ayahs: these were smells I had grown up with. I did not notice these smells any more in my teenage years than I had earlier on. Or if I noticed them, it was with the kind of familiar attention that I bestowed on the mango trees outside or on the evening moon floating like a thin cucumber slice in a lemonade sky. But lately I had become conscious of another kind of smell – that of women servants who were older than I was but not old. And with the consciousness of their smell came the realization of something other than odour. Their smells would draw me out of myself, send my imagination racing towards something else, make me yearn for, what? change? adventure? the clasp of firm, callused, gentle arms? sex?

Sex was too small a word for it. And I was not hypocritical enough to call it Love. Because while their smell penetrated the high invisible walls between people like me and people like them, they themselves entered my world, could enter my world only on invisible work permits. They were like Turkish immigrants in my eighties Germany: they had another skin (though sometimes the same colour), they spoke another language, they came from another place, they would never be given the citizenship to the lifestyle that came to me as a birthright. In some ways, what entered my world was their abstract labour power – and the smell that came along with it was deeply subversive for it indicated the existence of something else. They had smuggled in their bodies.

And it was Zeenat's smell that I felt most intensely. I would be unable to get it out of my head for hours; it would draw me to her as steadily, as rhythmically, as inevitably as the bucket that she drew up from the well when they ran short of municipal water.

How can I describe that smell? How can you describe the smell of a woman in her early twenties, of an average height and supple, firm build, a mother with a child dripping with snot and invariably neglected, a servant who had somehow managed to care for her appearance, who still put oil in her long black hair, sitting out in the sun, her rounded legs bare up to the knee and stretching out of a faded sari, who sometimes put jasmine flowers in her hair, who looked at you with an open, challenging stare, whose blouse wrenched your teenage eyes from other objects, making you notice anew every time its fullness and the sweaty dampness under her armpits?

7 –

The green water of the Kund beyond the Karbala-Kund turning. Two pilgrims, upper bodies bare, dipping their tonsured heads into it. Two of the older passengers lean out and toss 25-paisa coins at the Kund, fools, why don't they give it to him if they are loaded with the stuff, fucking old cunts. The coins do not carry so far. They fall by the roadside and in his side-view mirror he can see a group of children scrambling for them in the dust. They grow smaller and smaller, a blur of brown limbs, a commotion in the past.

A flock of doves lifts heavily from the road to make way for his bus. He sees them settling back again, waddling on the road, erasing his passage.

For a second, the image of Sunita comes to his mind: Sunita young, when her eyes had smiled at him and her lips had smiled at the world. Such a large flock of happiness had lifted from her face and eyes after marriage – or was it before marriage, when she decided, for she could have said no – such a large flock that never settled back. Never.

8 –

This is a town that knows apartments, though it has not become used to them. This is not Delhi or Bombay, with their apartment houses and multi-storeyed flats, their insulated cardboard boxes of privacy. This is not a city that has made up its mind about what to reveal and what to hide, what to enclose and what to expose. But neither is it Gaya or Phansa. It knows apartments and flats and the walls in-between; it knows the urban rituals of privacy. This is Patna: a city that is not quite a city, a town that is more than a town. Here there are walls between flats and houses, walls over which it is not always possible to peer, walls on which you cannot perch and hail your third cousin. But here the walls are still thin. They stretch like the membranes of your ear, fragile and more felt than seen. And, so often, they lie hidden in the deep recesses of your being. Here the walls are membranes through whose tight secrecy permeates much that may only be heard, not seen. It is this that sometimes makes you believe that you have heard all that needs to be heard.

That is why you sit in your flat on the third floor in

Kanchenjunga Apartments, the TV on but its sound switched off. A small symbol in one corner of your Philips screen attests to this watching that is not hearing: a trumpet-shaped image crossed out.

On the other hand, what you hear you do not need to see. You don't need to see the man walking up the stairway. The heavy tread of his footsteps, the regular intervals, the slight pause, like a sigh, after every fourth or fifth stair. You know these footsteps will continue to the flat right above you; these steps are Mr Sharma's.

No one in the building knows his first name. He is Mr Sharma, a junior-level officer in some government office in town. No one really knows which office; it is not one of those offices one needs to know. It is not the Electricity Department or PWD. That explains why no one knows Mr Sharma's first name. That explains why Mr Sharma wears a threadbare coat and is seriously worried about the marriage prospects of his three daughters.

You hear his heavy tread pass your door. He pauses and puts down something that rustles, picks it up again and proceeds climbing. You know that he is carrying a bag of wilting vegetables and fruits, bought from the roadside after long haggling, bought purposefully late in the day so that the seller would be willing to sell it cheap.

Above, there is a shuffling of feet in Mr Sharma's flat, a slight clanging of metal. Mrs Sharma has started busying herself in the small, soot-blackened kitchen with its one barred and netted window. There is the sound of a girl's voice repeating a few lines in English. This is the youngest daughter of the Sharmas, the one preparing for the first of the three ritual dips in the holy river of civil service exams. The eldest daughter has completed her three dips, twice getting beyond the preliminaries but no further, and has fallen into a morose silence that will, if Mrs Sharma is to be believed, soon be broken by the gaudy music of her marriage to a boy in 'gavernmint serbice'. The second daughter is going to try for the third time, but she has already lost the energy to recite her lessons aloud. She did not even make it beyond the preliminaries the first two times. Her silent studying is marked by querulous shouts, every hour or so, asking her mother to interfere and get the youngest sister to shut up. She is disturbing me, complains the second daughter. Go into the other room then, replies the mother instead. There are not that many rooms to go into in their flat. It is not a deluxe flat like the one you sit in or like Mrs Prasad's.

All sounds will cease momentarily when Mr Sharma rings the bell of the flat. Then the rhythm will pick up again, but on a lower key. Only Mrs Sharma will increase her share of the sounds: the sizzling and clanging in the kitchen will grow and the two older daughters will join their mother in preparing food for the evening meal. The youngest daughter will remain in the bedroom, cheap editions of guidebooks and 'keys' scattered around her, reciting her lessons in a soft murmur now.

You know the rhythms of their lives, including the

quarterly ritual of Mr Sharma's angina attacks. They are marked by a hush and then the scramble of slippered feet descending the stairs. One of the daughters, usually the eldest, knocks on your door or rings the bell of Mrs Prasad's flat next to you. Papa's had an attack, she gasps, Phone use kar saktey hain, please? The doctor is called. An hour lapses, filled with odd moans from Mr Sharma and absolute stillness in their flat. Sometimes, when it is warm and quiet outside, you can hear the soft flap-flap of Mrs Sharma or one of the daughters fanning the ailing man with a palm-leaf fan.

You hear a new pair of steps ascending the stairs, crisp, young, well-shod steps, and somehow the eldest daughter anticipates the arrival of the doctor and meets him two storeys down. He is ushered in and exits again in fifteen minutes, after a murmur of male voices with a few worried interjections by Mrs Sharma. This time Mrs Sharma escorts him to the landing, thanking him profusely, insisting on one of the daughters carrying his black leather medical bag to the Fiat below. Mrs Sharma's gratitude is sincere and blind to the fact that she has just paid the doctor a hefty fee. The doctor departs with soothing remarks and words like 'nothing serious, only rest for a day or two' and 'gastric attack'.

Chottu, Mrs Prasad's thirteen- or fourteen-year-old servant, goes up to enquire. He carries the news down to your landing, from where it is usually passed further down. A similar relay service carries the news up to the topmost flats on the sixth floor. Chottu is not the quickest of couriers though; he uses this opportunity to linger on various landings, gossiping with servants, women and children.

9 ~

The jeep has been blowing its horn for a couple of
minutes, like it is the driver's father's road. He looks in
the rear-view mirror, uncertain whether to let it pass or
continue obstructing it for a few more minutes, just for
the heck of it, he is driving the bigger vehicle, take it or
stuff it, bastard. What he sees makes him change his
attitude in a trifle. On the blunt wolf-like muzzle of the
jeep are the words:

Government of Bihar

DCM

TOYOTA

He pulls the bus to one side and the jeep jolts past,
horn still blaring, uniformed moustachioed men glaring
from its sides and back. Cunts.

10 –

By the standards of impoverished rural Bihar, Wazir Mian had accumulated a minor fortune in his years of service and, when I was eight, he decided to retire to his family and farm the land he had bought in his village. His wife, who had chosen to stay in their village home, had died a few years ago and his three sons were married men and had independent incomes now. He had a large family to look forward to and was obviously yearning to play the wise, retired patriarch.

As I said, things had changed in our compound as well by then: my grandfather had died and my father had built his own house, ghar, in one corner of the same compound, the rest of which had been sold in order to be distributed equally – and without litigation – between my grandfather's heirs; Wazir Mian's snow had long melted, and the hordes of guests who used to eat with my grandfather were neither around in such quantity nor as conveniently fed as in the past.

For three years, we heard nothing from Wazir Mian. Then he walked in one winter morning. There was dew on the grass and a faint touch of mist in the air. Mynahs were squabbling in the vegetable patch. We were sitting in the veranda, drinking tea. Wazir Mian lifted the latch of the metal gate and walked in, ignoring the sharp woofs of our Tibetan terrier, Tory. Tory, whose name had been corrupted from Thari (which reportedly means 'black' in Tibetan), took his role as the guardian of the family and the best friend of man very seriously. But Wazir Mian was not a person to be frightened by yapping lapdogs; he had worked in the compound when huge Alsatians were reared on dollops of boiled meat and bones. Ignoring Tory, he boomed a salaam to us and proceeded to where we were sitting on wicker chairs. He was older, slightly greyer, very slightly bent, a little thinner. He sat down on the top stair.

My father looked at my older brother and me, and we knew what we had to do. Wazir Mian was not only an old man but someone who had worked for my grandfather. He could not be allowed to sit on the floor. On the other hand, Wazir Mian was an old retainer, a man who believed in minute distinctions, and would refuse to sit on the same chairs as us. I ran in and got a stool for him to sit on. My father offered him the stool. Wazir Mian declined it elaborately. On cue, my mother repeated the offer, and Wazir Mian accepted the stool with an exaggerated show of physical relief. Then the conversation proceeded.

Papa: So, how are you, Wazir Mian?

Wazir Mian: Allah be praised.

Mummy: And your family, how are they?

Wazir Mian: Allah be praised.

Silence for a few seconds, as we drink tea. No one has offered Wazir Mian tea, knowing that he would not drink or eat in our presence. To offer him tea here would be a way of not offering him tea at all; he has to be offered tea in a manner and situation that is acceptable to him.

Wazir Mian: The babus have grown into young men since I last saw them.

Papa: Yes, one of them will be finishing high school soon.

Wazir Mian: Allah be praised.

Mummy: What about your sons, Wazir Mian? Didn't the eldest one have another child two years ago?

My mother had her contacts in the fleeting army of servants, ex-servants and their relatives who would visit to collect annual presents – mostly in cash – on the festival days that were important to them: Eid, Bakhr-eid, Holi, Diwali or Christmas. There were two or three who did their mite for Indian secularism and collected on all the festival days. Some of the more patriotic ones would turn up on Independence Day as well.

Wazir Mian: By the grace of Allah, he has a son and two daughters now.

Papa: You must be a busy grandfather.

Wazir Mian: Children are always a gift of Allah; it is the grown-ups who cause trouble.

Papa and Mummy exchange glances. More has been

said than my brother and I have heard. A servant is called in and asked to give Wazir Mian tea and snacks in the kitchen. Both my father and mother know that Wazir Mian is not on a short visit. He is here to stay.

The story came out only later, after Wazir Mian had resumed his tyrannical rule over our kitchen. It appears that the trouble started in his second year at the village. Wazir Mian, his fingers itching to cook elaborately, promised to do the Eid shopping and cooking for his joint family. He went to town and came back loaded with meats and ingredients. He trawled the village for the freshest vegetables. In the process, however, he spent five times more than the sum his sons had budgeted for.

His sons merely murmured about it, but his daughters-in-law complained loudly to the entire village. A man should know when to give in to age, said one of them to a neighbour. 'What does a man have to do in the kitchen?' another was supposed to have muttered. These comments were made in private, but nothing could be private in Wazir Mian's village. He was hurt when the comments were conveyed to him.

Perhaps provoked by the complaints, and because of his artist's attitude to cooking, Wazir Mian spent all of the next year skirmishing with his daughters-in-law about what should be cooked and how. He criticized their 'dehaati' cooking. They replied by pointing out that they were living in a 'dehaat' and not 'some laatsahab's palace'. He insisted on his right – as head of the family – to cook expensive dishes for his grandchildren. They contested that right.

Sooner or later, his sons had to interfere and Wazir Mian was effectively deprived of the patriarch's right to hold the family's purse strings. It was then that he had his final argument and left. He came back to the family that, he thought, would give him the chance to be the 'khansamah' that he was. Khansamah, a word that had been so full of connotations and nuances to Wazir Mian. Khansamah, a word that my brother and I had never heard used in any other family. A word gone out of fashion.

11 −

Plotted fields, mostly squares and rectangles, covered with thin green shoots and sprayed yellow flowers, fields of lehsun that look like an Impressionist canvas from a distance. No, if you asked him, he would not know what an Impressionist was, but, yes, he would inform you, there are books on art in Hindi and, for your information, son, he could read some gitpit English too, he could at least swear in it, damn you.

A mud track cutting across the fields and on the track a man in shirt and dhoti pushing his cycle. His cycle laden with four startlingly white sacks, pregnant pouches hanging on both sides of the metal frame. They make him think of the maalik, husband of his second cousin, Sunita, whom he had once hoped to marry, long ago, long long ago, they remind him of the maalik and his pregnant purses and he laughs aloud until tears come to his eyes, startling the passengers nearest to him. Just to reassure them, he clears his throat, balls together the phlegm in his throat and, leaning out of the window, expels it with such force that it falls clear across the road, in the dust, where it sizzles for a second and dissolves into a damp spot.

12 -

Chottu is still lingering outside. You can hear him chatting with one of the two servants from the Rais' double flat downstairs. It is almost seven and this is the time Mrs Prasad makes him sit down and do his homework. Mrs Prasad has to open her door and call him in.

Mrs Prasad seldom opens her door. Though she is invariably helpful and friendly with all the residents, the only person she sees regularly, apart from visiting relatives, is Dr Rai's wife from downstairs. Mrs Prasad's two sons and two daughters are married and settled in the big cities of India and abroad. They have done well; you can see their success reflected in the tasteful decor of the Prasad flat, the plush sofas and the profusion of hi-tech gadgets. You can even hear their affluence once in a while, when they come to visit and put on the CD player or switch on the huge TV in the sitting room. Mrs Prasad prefers watching the old black and white one in her bedroom. Mrs Prasad does not play music, though she watches Chitrahaar and other film-song programmes on her B&W television set. She also sits down to do her puja at seven thirty every morning and accompanies it with a bhajan in a hoarse, quavering, decidedly unmusical voice. She wakes you up every morning, but you have not thought of complaining. No one has.

13 ~

Entire walls of the low houses in many of the roadside villages have been turned into advertisements. Here most of them are painted yellow, bright yellow, and have lines and brand names written on them in red or blue.

BAIDYANATH, the first one announces. It is followed by PUJA GANJI AUR BANYAN and a wall full of illegible signs, freshly washed to make way for another ad. And then a smaller sign: UJALA TOOTHPOWDER, also in the Devanagari script.

14 -

Wazir Mian was among our literate servants. He wrote Urdu with some fluency and could calculate in Hindustani-Arabic numerals. But, specialist that he was of Mughlai and 'Continental' (European) cooking, he had his repertoire of English words as well. An entire army of secondary and high school teachers had to rinse some of his English words out of our mouths. Words like ishtake (steak), eesstoo (stew), chickun allah kaatey (chicken à la carte), tamater boss cat (tomato basket), karma puteen (caramel pudding), and they only managed to force my brother and me to abandon Wazir Mian's English in public. On private occasions, we continued – and we continue – to gorge ourselves on ishtakes and eesstoos. Steaks and stews taste so insipid. A delicately quivering, mouth-watering, lightly golden karma puteen continues to be the best proof we have ever had of the good deeds of our former lives.

But Wazir Mian – like most of the older servants and unlike most of the younger ones – did not ascribe much value to English. He never preferred an English word to its Urdu equivalent. And only once did he react to an English word spoken to him. It happened during a post-Bakhr-eid dinner party thrown for my father's friends.

At the end of the party, when Wazir Mian was taking his customary bow, my father introduced him to one of the guests – a South Indian officer who spoke very little Hindi or Urdu – in English. Wazir Mian did not understand the sentence, but he caught the key word: 'cook'.

What all of us had forgotten was that my brother had recently given Wazir Mian a short course in English. The course had been born out of Wazir Mian's desire to learn the English equivalent of a distinction that he had insisted on maintaining in Urdu. If he was ever introduced as the 'bawarchi' in Urdu, Wazir Mian would draw himself up to his full height of six feet or so and correct us: 'Not bawarchi, babu,' he would say in Urdu. 'Khansamah.' And recently he had learnt from my brother, who had simplified the matter a bit in a bid to give England a higher standing in Wazir Mian's esteem, that English had a similar distinction: 'cook' for 'bawarchi' and 'chef' for 'khansamah'.

Now catching 'cook' in my father's introduction and realizing that this time he could set matters right only in English, Wazir Mian gathered together all the English he had picked up cooking for regional princes, English officers and traditional-professional families like ours. He said with all dignity: 'No cook, sir, chieff.'

Even the mispronunciation had significance. As long as

Wazir Mian was around, there was no doubt who was the chief in the kitchen. In the realm of saucers, cups and chullahs, his authority was the final word – not only for his helpers but also for us and, most of the time, for our parents.

But the kitchen had started shrinking. Wazir Mian had been used to cooking in outdoor kitchens – separate rooms with a courtyard and storeroom attached. Now, of course, what we had was a one-room kitchen attached to the house. His helpers had disappeared too. There was less and less elaborate cooking for him to do. After the first month of Wazir Mian's return, when our parents gave him carte blanche to recreate dinners from the past and fill in gaps in our culinary experience, elaborate dinners petered out to about one every month. Most of the time, Wazir Mian had to make only two or three types of curry and one type of roti to go with it. On weekends he made sweet dishes. There were not enough people to eat his elaborate dinners – and the expense had gone up too.

Every other night, Wazir Mian would come out of the kitchen after serving dinner, cast a morose glance over the two or three dishes that were spread out on the dining table, and enquire, Can I be of any further service, Babu? No, that is not what he would say. He would say, like a genie released from the bottle, Kuch aur farmaish babu? Any other wish, Babu? His large hands would hang by his side, idle and restless. At times like this, I could sense something pass between my parents, something like irritation, which would make them snap at us if we did something even slightly unexpected. But they would answer Wazir Mian with careful politeness, Oh no, Wazir Mian, you have already done enough. A blank look would pass over Wazir Mian's face, as if he did not really understand the language my parents spoke, his large hands would hang even more heavily, and then he would turn and amble back into the kitchen.

Wazir Mian's children had been visiting him as well, all except his eldest son, looking sheepish the first time and bringing his grandchildren over every time after that. His grandchildren had missed him. After about eighteen months or so, Wazir Mian got a letter from home. Munnu is ill and his father wants some help back home, he told Ammi. Munnu was Wazir Mian's youngest grandson, a cheeky little fellow with a permanently runny nose and a dimple on the right cheek who was evidently a favourite of his grandfather. I will probably be back in time to cook for Eid, said Wazir Mian to my parents on his way to the bus stand.

He never came back, though he sent us succulent and delicious seekh kabab for Eid, wrapped in plastic and packed in an earthen pot. His eldest son, a thin man with a thinner moustache and an odd look of servile pride, came with it a few days before Eid. He had a two-inch scar on the left cheek, a dark oblong shape around a slight whitish ridge, the shape of the Milky Way. We knew that it was the result of a childhood fall.

It was the first time we had seen him since Wazir Mian's first departure. Abba is getting too old to work, he said apologetically, after bundling up the odds and ends that Wazir Mian had left behind in his room. He doesn't really need to, he added with a note of pride. And he ran a finger round the stiff collar of his new checked shirt, which, along with the terrycot bell-bottoms he wore, had probably been bought for Eid and put on to impress us with the undeniable fact of his upward mobility. His talk was also designed to prove to us that he was no peasant: he told us at least three times in ten minutes that they would be sacrificing an entire khassi this Eid and that he owned a 'raation shop' in the village. Though the dirt under his thick, cracked nails revealed that he did help out in the fields.

And when he enquired where the bus stopped, he stressed the word 'private'. He did not pronounce it 'preevaat' as most villagers do. But neither did he say 'private'. He said, with an excess of care that revealed how important this meagre knowledge of English was to him, how painfully aware he was of the deprivations of language and class, he said, 'priwait bus'.

15 ~

The shops at this stop are filled with cloth. There are retail shops, readymade-wear shops – children's frocks and shirts hanging on display – and tailors' stalls. The only shops that do not have something to do with cloth are the two medicine shops – one of them with a boxed-in clinic attached, featuring a doctor with degrees that are almost longer than the board with his name – and some tea and cigarette stalls. The biggest cigarette kiosk, perched on stilts, holds aloft a large, colourful board. CHARMS. The Taste That Sets You Free.

On the pavement squats a woman with a pile of makhana in front of her.

16 ~

With Chaand gone, I realized that I would not be able to pay the rent of our house. Our old kothi, inherited by our gharana, had been sold while our ustad was still alive. We had moved to a rented house in a back alley near the red-light area. It was not a pleasant area to live in. Every evening we would see the women hanging out from windows and doors, soliciting customers. During the nights, our sleep would be broken by drunken shouts and brawls. The police would find excuses to break in and search our house every month. And though the red-light area was the part of town that respectable, religious people ostensibly avoided in private life, it was also the part that received the greatest dose of public religion. Roman Catholic missionaries, the more liberal of the Jamait-e-Islami preachers, Hindu revivalists, almost everyone with a world to save came into this sink of moral vices to preach and condemn, save or damn. Recently, new religio-political parties had targeted our house for special attention – our intermingling of the Muslim and the Hindu was a constant thorn in their flesh, these days more so than our melange of the male and the female. This was not the way our ustad had lived or run her establishment in the past. We had been, shall I say, a very private 'public' house. So, the very next day, I quietly packed the VIP suitcase that I had and the large handbag that Chaand had given me, and stole out. I had to be careful, because there was a month's rent to pay, but I managed to walk down the alley and catch a rickshaw at the chowraha without being seen by the landlord or his family.

We had rented part of a large and crumbling house – once a talukdar's residence and now converted into seven flats. It was no longer anyone's home. The plywood partitions dividing the two immense halls between adjoining 'flats' ensured that. It was not even home to the landlord and his family, for they had long been dreaming of the time they would save up enough money to move to Patna. When I left the place it faded from my memory as easily as a photograph fades in the summer sunlight; if anything was left, it was the sepia tone of the caresses and gestures that I had shared with Chaand.

There was only one thing to do: I had to leave this town, the town I had grown up in. Istation chalo, I told the lungi-clad rickshaw puller. I had planned to buy a train ticket to the neighbouring town, Phansa. I had been to Phansa only once for a nautch-show and felt that I could get ordinary work there without being haunted by my past. Quite frankly, I wished for a job. I wanted to live like a woman and not like a eunuch. The life of a eunuch these days was too degrading for me. Moreover, I feel more like a woman. If I were forced to choose, I would rather be a woman than a man. You may even say I look like a woman: I am slight in build and have striking dark eyes, full lips and a fine aquiline nose. I have long, thick hair, falling down to my waist, the envy of most women. My arms are perhaps more veined than is usual among middle-class women in these parts, but I have seen peasant women with leathery, more muscular arms. Dressed in a sari, no one can take me for a eunuch.

At the station, though, I was told that all trains running to Phansa had been cancelled. A maalgaadi had derailed somewhere on the Gaya–Phansa line, covering the tracks with the scrap metal and coal that it had been transporting. It was too late, now, to go back to the kothi, and I did not wish to catch a public bus; they are usually overcrowded and would be even more so with the trains not running. There was no option but to invest part of my meagre savings – or, rather, part of the unpaid monthly rent – in booking a more expensive place on a private bus. More expensive, but not necessarily better, as I was to find out. I caught another rickshaw to the corner outside the government bus stop where the private buses stopped. Having bought a ticket from the surprisingly courteous conductor of a bus that had already started revving its engine, I was about to climb into it when I was recognized by an old patron of our house. It was Iskander Mian, an old man, paan-stained, hairless, with a face that was like a dry date, a chhuara.

What, what, what, Farhana Begum? he said, limping towards me. Where are you going? You are not leaving us all alone with a broken heart, are you?

Like all men who had come to our gharana, Iskander Mian had to call me 'begum': he lacked the courage to utter the truth of my male surname.

I am sorry, I replied in as cold a voice as I could muster. You are mistaken. My name is Parvati.

And before he could react I boarded the bus, with the conductor courteously stowing away my suitcase and even showing me to a seat. When the bus started moving a minute later, Iskander Mian was still standing there, looking confused, a few more lines on his chhuara face. Just as we pulled out on to the road, however, the bus stopped and my heart leapt to my mouth. I could visualize Iskander Mian and the landlord, accompanied by all the clients we had ever known, boarding the bus, pleading in their half-mocking tone, do not break our hearts, Farhana, do not leave us all alone in this wide wide world.

I was relieved when a woman carrying a bundle and a snivelling child got on and the bus started moving again with a loud meshing of gears.

17 –

He notices the white heap of makhana with its black spots. If you focused closely enough you would only see whiteness speckled with black, a clear night's sky inverted.

Makhana is the popcorn of Bihar, he thinks. Except that it is tastier and crisper. They say it is only grown in the Darbhanga, Purnia, Saharsa and Madhubani districts of North Bihar. No Hindu or Muslim marriage can take place without it, though very few Hindus or Muslims know where it comes from. Very few Hindus and Muslims know anything except where they themselves come from and they have mostly got that wrong anyway. They do not know how it is planted by mallahs in the months of March and April. It is planted in ponds at a depth of six to eight feet. The thorny plant that emerges from the water has large leaves, large enough for water birds like the long-legged chaha to perch on them. About six months after it has been planted, the gudi fruits, which hang under the large flat leaves, ripen and fall to the bottom of the pond. Mallahs dive into the water and bring the fruits up by the bucket, their dark, thin bodies encrusted with leaves and roots. The fruit is dried and then it is roasted and beaten until it bursts into lavva or makhana. It is this makhana that one can buy from the roadside, fried and sprinkled with pepper and salt. One does not need to know where it comes from or how much effort has gone into making it. If one has the money, one only needs to know how much it costs. It does not cost much. Not a fraction as much as popcorn packets in dark and damp cinema halls.

18 ~

A middle-aged man in white banyan and checked lungi came out of the shop carrying a stainless steel bucket. Water slopped out of the bucket. With practised gestures, the man dipped his hands into the bucket and scattered arcs of water around him. The drops fell on the dry dust of the roadside, spotting it at first, then drawing ropes on it, ropes of water that the man hoped would keep it tied down through the first hours of morning traffic. A metal board above the shop said 'Manohar Sweets' in English and then below it, in smaller Hindi, 'yahan shudh ghee ki swadisht mithaiyan milti hain'.

'Ghasmus-sir, sorry, sir, two minute, two minute,' shouted the driver from a window next to the mithai shop.

Rasmus adjusted his six feet two inches on the back seat of the off-white Ambassador, making sure that one of his hands rested on the thin attaché case next to him. The attaché case – or rather its contents – was weighing on Rasmus's conscience, making him more irritable than usual, more conscious of time and place. He watched the mithai man fetch another pail of water. Rasmus had been in Gaya long enough to know that this particular street, leading out to the road to Patna from which you turned off at Tehta to go to Phansa, had once been known for its tilkuts. But even if Rasmus had not spent a few weeks in Gaya, he would have known about tilkut. Tilkut was the mithai that Gaya had contributed to the multiple cuisine of North Indian sweets. He could hear his father's voice filling with sunshine and syrup as he spoke of Indian mithais on a rainy, overcast day in Copenhagen. Go to any old North Indian village or town, mister, and you will discover a local mithai, made only or in a distinctive way in that place. Khirmohan in Dhoda, khaja in Silao, tilkut in Gaya. His father could go on and on about Indian food in Copenhagen, often with the kind of intensity that made Danes, and sometimes Rasmus, fidget in their chairs.

A few mithai shops were still left on the street – including two or three with the clear space and wooden pole that one needed to twist and turn the dough for making tilkut – but most shops had started stocking more profitable and durable commodities. The man went in, still leaving a few areas of dry dust around his shop. A newspaper vendor cycled past. Rasmus could hear the loud, rasping noise of someone clearing his throat in the house next door: the loud, multi-layered, many-sided sound of a man performing his morning ablution in the traditional way. It was not even eight in the morning, and few people were on the street. However, Rasmus could sense the bathrooms and kitchens coming to life, and a small crowd had started collecting around the municipal tap further down the road, waiting for the water to come on with a sputter at eight thirty or so. He leaned forward and blew the Ambassador's horn – a short, polite but urgent sound. Rasmus's time-rhythm was already upset. India always disturbed his finely tuned, many-quartz inner watch. That was perhaps what he found most disruptive about his occasional stays in India, troubleshooting for the head office in Copenhagen. He never felt that way in Tokyo, Bangkok or Abu Dhabi. The Middle East and the Far East, he thought, mostly danced to the tick-tocking of a Western clock, but India, India followed a hundred different clocks or none at all. He blew the horn again, more insistently this time.

Bajao horn, bajao horn, muttered Hari, glancing out of his window at Rasmus in the Ambassador. Pura nashta kar kay chalengay: yeh koi firangistan thoday hi hai! But despite his brave words, he hurriedly gobbled the last mouthful of chappati and bhunjiya, shouted at his wife to make sure that Munna went to school and stumbled out of the door muttering. Because he could not really shout at Rasmus, he shouted more loudly at his wife than he needed to.

Last time I let you stop for breakfast at home, said Rasmus, when Hari opened the door of the car. You said ten and took twenty minutes, mister.

The 'mister' slipped out unexpectedly: once again his father, who would 'mister' him when in a hectoring mood, once again his father's ghost, exorcised so many times, entering by his mouth.

Sorry, sir, sorry, life-partner never hear, what to say, replied Hari in English. He revved the Ambassador's engine and released the clutch with a shuddering rasp that, Rasmus was still to discover, was always a critique of his employer's strict sense of time. The Ambassador sped through the space watered down by the mithai man, obliterating some of his watery designs and setting in sequence the pattern of his day. The man had hitched up his lungi and was busy rinsing one of the big cauldrons in the veranda of his shop. Settling the dust every morning was a ritual for him, an act that joined his days together. He knew that two hours later he would be twisting and turning his strands of tilkut dough out in the open, the sticky stuff filling with the sweetness of the family recipe and the dust of cars, rickshaws, thellas, cycles, pedestrians.

19 ~

A black Rajdoot motorcycle overtakes his bus. It is being steered by a man in a khaki safari suit. His seven- or eight-year-old son straddles the long seat behind him and his wife is perched, both legs on one side, behind the son.

The motorcycle wobbles dangerously and regains its balance, the woman readjusts the pallu on her head with an automatic hand. Soon they are a dwindling speck on the long and narrow road. Above them, the sky stretches like a blue marble tabletop in some roadside restaurant, wiped by some serving boy with a dirty rag dipped in watery white phenol.

20 -

I would take her smell with me to bed. Though when she looked at me, I would fail to sustain the look. Her eyes would wrestle mine to the ground, and then her lips would curl with the shadow of a smile. And she would greet me in a voice of servile humility: Salaam-alai-kum, Irfan babu. Walai-kum-assalaam, Zeenat, I would stutter back.

Peace was the last thing Zeenat could bestow on me.

She worked at a neighbour's house, the only substantial kothi in our increasingly congested neighbourhood in New Karimganj, an old house, once great now crumbling, once prosperous now pretentious. It was a house of many rooms; most of them boarded up now. It had been built for a joint family. I remembered an extended family flitting through it during summer holidays in my child-hood. Now it was inhabited by a shifty-eyed lawyer, his wife and four daughters, and his aunt, a broad-boned, paan-chewing woman with faint whiskers and flapping old-fashioned clothes that underlined her claim to the house.

The lawyer had come to live with his aunt and look after the house when her son was shot dead by unknown persons – some said accidentally during a road hold-up and others said because of a failed business venture. She had herself gone on with life after the period of mourning, refusing to sell off the house and move in with her daughters in Delhi. And it was only because of repeated phone calls by her daughters, who would periodically imagine her falling down the stairs or wasting away unattended, that she had finally allowed her lawyer nephew to move into a section of the house.

But the house hung loose on the nephew's shoulders. Every other week we heard his voice raised and squeaky in argument, quelled finally by the obdurate, monosyllabic responses of his aunt. He wanted to let out parts of the house. Not until I am dead, said the aunt. Then, later, she would sit on the veranda and mumble about what the house had been, how many guests they had fed every day, how many poor relatives they had brought over from the ancestral village and sent to local schools, how many servants had scurried from kitchen to dining room, bearing food on large silver trays.

Zeenat was the last maidservant left in the house. They still had two male servants though, including an old rickshaw puller. All servants except the lean and leathery rickshaw puller were new to the house, hired by the lawyer and liable to change every year or so. Only the puller had been there earlier, and he was still there, plying the family rickshaw, taking the daughters to school and bringing them back, taking the wife shopping and the lawyer to the crowded district courts, and sometimes taking the aunt, paandaan attached to a stand welded into the rickshaw, purdah draped across the hood, taking the aunt to some surviving old relative's kothi in old Karimganj.

But Zeenat was the only servant I noticed. Sitting there, peering out from the rooftop of my parents' house, I had a grand view of our neighbours' courtyard. That is where Zeenat and the other servants lived: Zeenat in a room attached to the main house, next to the stairs, the male servants in rooms further off, on the other side of the courtyard. I would watch her sitting there winnowing the rice or, during an extended power cut, drawing water from the well in the courtyard. I would watch her after a bath, drying out her hair in the sun. And just once or twice I thought she smiled her knowing ghost of a smile in my direction and, in the same gesture, demurely covered her head with the sari pallu and carelessly bared a leg to the knee.

I had to be careful on the roof. I had to remember to rush back into my room below before replying to an unexpected summons by my parents. My parents did not tolerate Peeping Toms, partly because the term did not exist in their chaste Urdu, and Zeenat was not a favourite either. My parents found her 'brazen' and 'wanton'. They were both teachers – my father in the local Mirza Ghalib

College and my mother in Nazareth Academy – and their notions of propriety were strict and pedagogic. Once my father suggested, in euphemisms I was not supposed to understand, that Zeenat had probably been a whore. He did not say 'whore', he preferred 'tawaif', with its softening connotations of music and culture. My father considered it a mark of the lawyer's lack of character that Zeenat – that 'tawaif', that 'street woman' – continued to be employed in such a respectable old 'house'. There was a controversy when I suggested, with sarcasm born of repressed teenage hormones and a budding quasi-leftist view of respectability, that tawaifs had a perfectly logical relationship to old 'houses', respectable old 'houses' in particular.

21 ~

A pond or a trough from which the monsoon water would not evaporate most years. On its banks, three ragged banana bushes and behind them a number of hunched huts made of bricks and mud, the walls facing the road unplastered but chalked white. Beyond it all the biggest, tallest Sita Ashok tree he has ever seen. He notices this tree on every trip. It is said that if you drank the water in which its delicate, perfumed flowers had been washed, you would be cured of grief.

Those were the days when grief must have been a mud hut, Mangal Singh thinks with a twisted smile. Easily erected from the earth, easily washed away by the floods. Now we make our grief of concrete and cement, steel and iron: we inhabit its empty room.

22 –

Everyone I had ever known and cared for had gone out of my life with the departure of Chaand. I must say, I did not have a clear idea of what I would do when I reached Phansa; perhaps work as an ayah. I merely wished to leave our town and start all over again. But things took a turn of their own. Things, as our old tabla player and music teacher used to say, always take a turn of their own. It is people who never take a turn of their own, never, never, poor prisoners, kunji-maar, turn-key bastards that we have become, he would sometimes add, harsh laughter and the coughs of terminal TB bursting out of him at the same time.

Sitting on the weathered, torn seats of the bus, looking at the rest of the passengers from the corner of my eye, for our seat was a side one, feeling the bus swell with body heat and odours even though it was a pleasant day outside, sitting there as fields and hamlets hobbled by, I replied silently to him as I had that day, too. I said I will take a turn of my own when the time comes, mark my words, I will take a turn when things take a turn.

In the bus, I sat next to an old woman who was also going to Phansa. Actually, the conductor had insisted that I should sit next to her, and later I realized why. The conductor was trying his utmost to please the old woman, and he had ensured that the seats around her were occupied by women, and as urbane-looking ones at that as could be managed on a bus like his.

The old woman was in her early sixties, which is old in these parts, but she was sharp and alert. She somehow resembled a mynah, though she was by no means a small bird. A raucous mynah, alert and sharp. That was the first thing I remarked about her, because of the way she haggled with the tea-boy through the railings of the bus window. She managed to browbeat him into charging her only fifty paisa for a cup of ispayshull chai that would have cost one rupee. You should never let these chokkras take advantage of you. They are pickpockets, all of them! she told me after the tea-boy went away, grumbling. I agreed for the sake of politeness.

By the way she haggled, one would have thought she was poor. But her language and her clothes did not indicate any poverty. She was wearing a white sari – which obviously meant that she was a widow. However, it was not a plain cotton sari. It was of some richer material, with off-white embroidery around the borders, and it looked new. Only rich people wear new clothes when they are travelling by bus or train in this state. The trains on this route do not have a first-class compartment and the buses are even more democratic; you have to travel like the masses, and that soils your clothes. I could also see her hand baggage, jammed under the bench. It was expensive; not even VIP or Aristocrat, it looked imported. It was evident that she belonged to another social class from the rest of us sitting behind the partition of the driver's seat, where three extra seats had been welded into the floor to form a square open on one side. It had been effectively turned into a section reserved for women. There were other women in the bus, of course, but – like the woman with a snivelling child sitting just behind our section – they were obviously not respectable enough to be given seats away from men. There were seven of us in the section.

One woman wore a purdah, though she had lifted the veil inside the bus. Three of the others wore relatively clean but crumpled cotton saris while the fifth was a ten-year-old, pony-tailed girl dressed in a torn frock. She was accompanying one of the women, probably her mother. Apart from the old woman, I was the only person who was wearing rather prosperous-looking clothes. I had a shalwar-kameez on, with a flowery print. An old dress, but unpatched and clean, freshly pressed. Perhaps that is why the old woman spoke a lot to me throughout the trip. But then, she spoke a lot in general, in a polite and only slightly condescending manner. She appeared to feel that she had to speak to us in order to bridge the gap that her obvious affluence might create. Moreover, she was a

strong, opinionated person. Starting from the initial statement about the tea-boy, she diverged into the virtues of
saving (which included a categorical refusal to own a car
or travel by taxi) and then ended up telling us about
her earlier poverty and her political beliefs, which were
rightist-Hindu.

We were refugees from Lahore, she had told us even
before we reached the first stop. When we reached Delhi
on 27 October 1947, all we had was a thousand and fifty-
two rupees in cash and my jewels. People of my generation know what it means to save. Not like the new
generation. Give them a hundred rupees and they spend
it in a day. Give them a thousand, and they spend it in a
day too. The more you spend, the more you get, says my
son to me. That is easy for you to say, I told him, you
will always have money thanks to your father, may-god-
give-peace-to-his-soul. If you had only a thousand rupees
left and were in a new country, you would lose all desire
to spend!

What did you do then, mother? asked the woman
accompanied by the ten-year old girl. How did you
survive?

We lived in a refugee camp for six months, getting our
food ladled out to us in the common kitchen. Then, god
be praised, we were allotted a house in East Delhi. It was
a bad locality, there hardly used to be houses in East
Delhi in those days. This house had been vacated by a
Muslim family, which had fled to Pakistan. You know,

that is how it was in those days: houses emptied by Muslims in India were given to us and our houses were given to those Muslims in Pakistan. Someone told me later that our old house in Lahore – it had seven rooms – is now occupied by a Muslim cobbler from somewhere. Just think, a cobbler, a Muslim cobbler! Anyhow, we shared this house with another refugee family. They took the upper floor and we occupied the ground one. Both the floors had two bedrooms, one large and one small. But we still did not have any money. My husband – he passed away four years ago – was nine years older than me, and it was harder on him. He had to start all over again. Back in Lahore, he had a garments shop, a very successful one. In Delhi, he had only a thousand rupees to start with, and some no-good relatives. I sold off my jewels – everything except the mangalsutra – and he entered the clothes retail business. That provided us with our daily bread, but it was not enough. We could not afford some basic amenities. I bought my first new sari only two years after we came to Delhi. Vijay, my son, could not be sent to a good English-medium school for two years or so. It was a hard life. That is why we learnt the importance of saving. I keep on telling this to Vijay, but he only laughs. The good Lord giveth and the good Lord taketh away, blessed be the name of the Lord, he says. All this English education!

She noticed the look of mild incomprehension on our faces. Her easy switch to English had left us in the dark.

I could ragpick two or three words from her fluent sentence, the others probably not even that. The old woman gave a short, embarrassed cough and explained. It sounds impressive in Angrezi, doesn't it, but it simply means what we can say in five words – Sab Bhagwan ki leela hai.

This reminder of the social gulf between her and us made her pause, and when she resumed she adopted a slightly more conservative stance, an enlightened and nationalist conservatism, as if to tell us that deep down she did not differ from us, that deep down she shared our 'Indian' values. It was surprising how easily we acquiesced in her construction of a plural identity, for of course the woman in purdah would have said, 'Sab Allah ke haath hai,' and I might have said, 'Sab lekhni ka khel hai,' and who knows what particular divinities the other women would have invoked?

Momentarily, though, the old woman broke her account to look out of the window as we wended our way out of the stop at Bela, apparently swimming in a narrow stream of rickshaws and thellas, the conductor hanging out of the back door, banging the sides of the bus and shouting curses at cyclists and pedestrians. He was a different man with us, though. He would come to enquire after the old woman and once when she said that he need not bother so much, he protested that it was no bother. Your son, maaji, is not only my maalik's very good friend, he is also a naami man. The only good thing about the derailment of the maalgaadi is that this poor bus has had the fortune of bearing your sandals. The least I can do is serve you while you are here, he said.

A courteous man the conductor, at least around us, though I could hear him being harsh and even abusive – employing the rough 're' as a generic mode of address – with the really rustic passengers. Not with all of them, for the Indian People's Front and the Communist Party of India (Marxist-Leninist) are active in the villages of these areas. He was abusive only with those who were evidently not the sort who could be card-carrying members of revolutionary parties, or gun-carrying members of gangs.

23 –

As Mangal Singh sips the chai at the bus stop, slurping to cool it down occasionally, he thinks of that drink which could cure grief. Tall order that one: not TB, not cancer, not even AIDS but sister-fucking grief. He was once told why the Ashoka's flowers had that property. A passenger, an old sadhu, withered and appropriately white-bearded, born the colour of night or burnt black in the sun, had told him the story.

He is reminded of the story by a group of villagers walking past. The group contains two or three aborigines – tribals, is what he calls them. They are now out in that overlooked part of the state, beyond the Dhoda stop, where tribals can still be seen sometimes, and seen in circumstances that do not clothe their semi-naked tribalness in urban trousers or pyjamas. Seen in their dark skins and their torn loincloths, their individual pride and their collective poverty. Why has the cure not worked on them?

It was a tribal named Sashoka who had been granted the boon of turning into that tree from whose branches mighty Hanuman would console the abducted and desolate Sita, yes, her again, her of the curse. Hanuman would console her, the mistress of the curse, from its branches and hence, hey presto, Ashoka, the griefless tree. Why is it then, he wonders, that the descendants of Sashoka still wander around hugging their small bundles of grief?

24 -

'Why don't you sell this junk and get yourself a Maruti?'

Hari felt insulted by the question, blew his horn hard at an intransigent thella and chose not to reply. He could have replied though. He could have retorted, And how do you think you would fit your nine feet into a dingy Maruti? That retort came to his lips in pidgin English but he swallowed it.

Hari had got his job – and a lucrative job it was, one that paid almost three times what he would have earned elsewhere – because of his ability to understand and speak English. He was one of the two or three drivers in Gaya who could understand English. All of them had learnt English in the course of driving tourists around in Bodh-Gaya, for the schools they had attended either taught no English or did so just on paper. Of the lot, Hari was most fluent in English – far more fluent, actually, than he let on. He had worked as a tourist guide in Bodh-Gaya and Nalanda, which had made him pick up more words of English than most drivers required. Still, his best tourist language was not English but Japanese. Japanese tourists came to the area more often – for this was the historical heartland of Buddhism – and haggled less than Western tourists. Quite a number of the unemployed, shady young men who drifted around Bodh-Gaya and combined petty smuggling with seasonal 'guide services' spoke Japanese with various degrees of competence and imagination. A decade back some would have known Thai as well, but that language was dying out with the decline of the Tiger economies.

Hari had understood every word of what Rasmus had said. He had even understood its tone, which was the reason he had pretended not to understand the comment. Rasmus was irritated – irregular time and the contents of his attaché case were weighing on him – and, as such, he was being sarcastic. Hari had a theory of the irritation of the nationalities: the Americans would get loud and abrasive, the Japanese would become politer but obstinate, the Scots and the English would tend to lecture you on various universal (Scottish and English) values, the French would remonstrate and then tip you significantly less, the Germans would either swallow their irritation with a conscious effort or bluster, the Danes would make indirect comments of criticism. Of the lot, Hari preferred the French response, for he appreciated its honestly economic logic.

It is strange, thought Hari, as he blew the horn loud enough to dissuade an old man from crossing the street, it is strange that however much he might laugh at Ambassadors with his friends, he did not want these trusty models to be criticized by his customers, especially those from outside India. He felt like retorting to Rasmus, well, at least we make our own cars. But he kept quiet out of professional deference and because he did not know enough about Denmark. Perhaps they made their own cars there as well. All he knew about Denmark was that they produced lots of milk. 'Land of milk and butter you come from, sir, no?' he had said to Rasmus on the day he was being interviewed for the 'contract job', knowing that in its clownish semi-knowledge the question would be good public relations. Its subtle blend of information and ignorance would tend to reassure the sahab. It had worked. But the reason why Hari associated Denmark with milk and butter had to do with a faint childhood recollection: of a photograph showing an immensely fat and smug-looking white-spotted-with-brown cow. Hari had earlier supposed that the picture depicted a scene from France – that was when he had been hired for a semester by a visiting French archaeologist – but now he was certain that it depicted Denmark. It was the smug expression on the cow's face that clinched the argument for Hari after he got to meet a couple of Danes. Apart from that, he had no way of knowing whether Denmark produced milk or petroleum. And he was not particularly bothered as long as Rasmus produced his salary – and the occasional advance – on time.

Readjusting himself on the plastic front seat of the Ambassador, Hari thought of repeating his comment in a more aggressive form ('Denmark produce nothing but milk, sir, no?'), but then he got distracted by a twittering flock of sparrows hopping from window sills and shop boards to the roadside and felt his irritation ebb away. They were not that much behind schedule, anyway. He could be tolerant with Rasmus's usual jibes. He knew that Rasmus had an important appointment with the state agriculture ministerji, who could help him land a contract for his multinational company. The ministerji was also the MP from Phansa, and hence their trip today.

Hari would be tolerant. He was used to Rasmus, to Ghasmus-sir as he addressed him, unable to pronounce the Danish 'r', or to Ghasphus-sir as he referred to him back home. Not that tall, broad-shouldered, healthy-looking Rasmus resembled the kind of straggly grass and weeds that people referred to as ghasphus.

25 -

Suddenly out of nowhere on a broken wall the scrawled graffiti in Devanagari: Proust Padho!

Read Proust.

What, he wonders, is fucking Proust?

26 −

They were crawling through the narrow street of Karbala-Kund, which used to be a detached village but had now become the last 'suburban' area of Gaya. This was the tricky part, and one of the many reasons for Rasmus's irritation. There was a curve in the road ahead at exactly the point where the road bottlenecked even further, so much so that it allowed only one vehicle through at a time. Rasmus was aware that trucks and buses started plying from nine in the morning. Rasmus − and Hari, though he would not concede it − wanted to be out of this part before the morning congestion built up.

It was turns like this one that made the Ambassador a sensible choice, Hari told Rasmus silently in his mind. A single scratch on the Maruti from a pushy truck and you would have to spend a minor fortune getting it repaired. And wait until you come to the first proper speed breaker, the huge ones that villagers construct on their own outside their villages. In a Maruti it would be a car breaker.

A bearded, garlanded picture of Sai Baba dangled from the rear-view mirror of the Ambassador and sagely nodded in agreement with Hari's sentiments. The Ambassador, off-white paint flaking off in a few places, hobbled along the narrow road. Hari changed into a lower gear, more gently and with no noise this time. He had entered the bottleneck curve and could see a truck entering from the other end. They were still more than a hundred yards apart. Hari stepped on the accelerator and shot the Ambassador ahead in low gear. He could see the truck spurt forward as well. Rasmus, who after a moment of shocked silence started expostulating, attributed this rash game of chicken to the obstinacy and myopic vision of the drivers and the lack of traffic rules on Indian roads. But Hari and the truck driver were adhering to a strict if unspecified code. They knew that the vehicle that got furthest into the curve would be given the right of passage. Even as they screeched to a halt merely a metre from each other, Hari could see that the race had not ended in a definite result. Both the vehicles were about halfway into the curve. Still, he ignored Rasmus's complaints and stuck out his head to remonstrate with the truck driver.

The truck driver refused to budge. He had read the unwritten book of local traffic rules quite thoroughly: in an undecided contest, the smaller vehicle had to give way. Grumbling about 'bloody-fool Indian drivers, sir', Hari backed all the way and watched the truck driver roar past him with a nonchalant wave.

Rasmus was still protesting and Hari thought it best to defuse the tension by exploiting his employer's earlier prejudice. 'Ambassador car old-junk car, sir, move like lame tortoise,' he said, feeling worse than Judas. 'I sell coming year, buy Maruti van.' He was not particularly worried about Rasmus's complaints – in spite of getting miffed once in a while, Rasmus was an indulgent employer. Neither did he think much about Rasmus's views on Indian things and habits, though Rasmus was the first European he had met who understood Hindustani and even spoke some. Back in the company office, there had been some rumours about his father having been an Indian – but Rasmus did not look Indian to Hari. As for Rasmus's understanding of Indian practices, why, hadn't Hari just seen him stop to correct the workers setting up a tent next to the company office? It was a marriage tent and the workers were following an illogical and circuitous procedure that significantly increased the number of hours they would spend working on it. Rasmus had stopped to explain a simpler method to them, not even imagining – what was clear to Hari – that the workers were purposefully increasing the number of hours they worked and got paid for. 'More logical,' he had muttered while explaining it to the workers, who had looked suitably impressed. It was, however, a very illogical kind of logic for the workers who had returned to their old method the moment Rasmus left. No, Hari was not particularly impressed by Rasmus's logic – or at least not as impressed as he was by Rasmus's elaborate zoom-lens camera.

But they still had almost two hours to go before they reached Phansa, and Hari did not want to drive with Rasmus finding fault with him from the back seat. He felt that this was one of those days when he could not bear too much criticism. He held up an olive branch. 'No good car, Ambassador car, sir,' he said, swallowing his pride in the Ambassador and negotiating the curve with greater caution. The streets had already started filling up. A couple of vegetable vendors were setting up stalls. Women were walking up with agricultural and dairy produce balanced on their heads. Students, some dressed in the faded imitation uniforms of cheap private schools, were on their way to classes in tin-roofed rooms and on cemented verandas.

27 –

Labourers standing in the sun, holding crowbars and shovels. They are working on the adjoining single-gauge railway track. Further on, a white government Ambassador is parked next to a gullar tree and some officers are standing in the shade of its spreading branches. It is not so warm outside as to force one to seek the shade, but of course the heat has nothing to do with it.

Even above the sounds of the road and the humming of his engine, he hears the hollow call of a pigeon.

28 ~

There is the sound of film music coming from Mrs Prasad's flat. It is switched off. It is time for Chottu's lessons. Mrs Prasad believes in education; her children are living embodiments of what education can get you. Her husband, god bless him, worked in various banks and saved all his life in order to get their children the best possible education: top English-medium missionary schools in Patna and then directly to Delhi University. In his memory, she sends Chottu to 'English classes' run by one of the wives in an adjoining apartment building.

Chottu does not see much point in getting an education. He is no fool. Since he was first brought to Mrs Prasad's by his villager parents at the age of eight or nine and left there on the agreement that 75 per cent of his salary would be money-ordered to his father every month, he has grown to understand and know this new urban world. He knows more people in the neighbourhood than Mrs Prasad does. He is no longer the small, timid boy, dressed in a ganji and half-trousers, mucus peeping out of one nostril between sobs. He dresses as smartly as he can and carries a comb all the time. He has a collection of cheap sunglasses, mostly of plastic, which Mrs Prasad always makes him take off. His voice has started breaking. He sometimes sits with older boys at the nukkad and gambles with the 25 per cent of his salary that is given to him. He feels that education is something not really for the likes of him. He has the example of the chaalloo nukkad boys who have come into money. He has the example of young men and women, like the eldest Sharma daughter, who have rigorously studied themselves into a future of self-doubt, frustration and failure. He knows all the school masters and professors in the neighbourhood, and has discovered that the ones with money are the ones with other sources of income than those bestowed on them by their degrees. He doubts that Mrs Prasad's sons have made their money the straight and narrow way. He has seen Hindi films. He knows all about easy money, though he has never had any. He wonders whether anyone who has had to study and struggle for money would buy a gleaming new air-conditioned Contessa and leave it in the garage for occasional use, once a year or so, during visits. That is what Mrs Prasad's eldest son did when he was in town from Chicago almost two years ago. And the CD set and huge imported TV that Mrs Prasad never wanted and refuses to use.

Chottu sees the world quite clearly, though tinted one fixed shade by his own deprivation, as if he were wearing a pair of plastic sunglasses all the time.

Chottu makes a point of disappearing right when Mrs Prasad is about to call him to do his homework. Home-burk-shomeburk, you have heard him mutter. Mrs Prasad calls, Chottu, Chottuu, Chotttuuuu, her voice sounding more peeved with each call. There is no response. You can hear Mrs Prasad shuffling to the door and then to the grilled landing. Chottu, Chottuu, Chotttuuuu, she shouts into the dark night. There is the sound of traffic and even a faint lapping of water from the Ganges at a distance. The river is still full after the recent monsoon. Mrs Prasad shouts again, peering into the darkness below, the cement-bordered park that only holds a few bushes and already yellowing grass, the cars parked below reflecting the yellow of two 40-watt street bulbs, one of the bulbs attached to a loose socket and swinging in the slight breeze, throwing furtive shadows over Fiats, Ambassadors, Marutis, over flats with barred windows glazed a low-wattage yellow, like jaundiced eyes, or gleaming with the white of mercury tubes.

You hear a sizzle in the flat above. Mrs Sharma has thrown thinly sliced onions into boiling ghee: she is in the last phase of preparing dinner. Soon the tarka will be ready and poured into the daal. There will be rice and a vegetable curry to go with it. Pickles. There will be pappads, perhaps. You haven't smelled the pappad yet or heard it sizzle. The Sharmas eat early.

Mrs Prasad is now calling the durban appointed by the housing cooperative and installed in a shed next to the gate. The durban responds at the fourth call. His voice is slurred and muffled: either the consequence of an early glass of toddy or of the dirty grey chaddar that he wraps around himself at the slightest sign of chill in the air. The durban is instructed to get Chottu; Mrs Prasad closes her door a bit more loudly than usual.

Outside you can hear the town, the city. There is the low drone of an aeroplane, one of the few using the local airport. The Ganges is louder now, because the traffic noises have faded slightly. People are home watching TV, only the odd car or truck passes the apartments. There are occasional bursts of irritated honking from a distance: some roads are too narrow or still crowded. There is a record playing in the distance. You know it's a record because it gets stuck every once in a while. Probably an early wedding, you think. The wedding season has not really begun yet. When it does, there will be a cacophony of film music and inane, sexually suggestive pop songs followed by occasional outbursts of complaint from Mrs Prasad next door. Mrs Prasad can watch without complaint film stars grating their hips together and thrusting over-dressed pelvises at each other in a manner that leaves little to the imagination, but the slightest bit of nudity or verbal obscenity rouses her ire.

You hear light reluctant steps climbing the staircase, keys being trailed jangling against the metal railing.

The Sharmas are already sitting down to eat: there is the sound of metal folding chairs being dragged into place, aluminium plates being laid. The youngest daughter has stopped learning by rote.

Mrs Prasad's door opens and closes.

You have heard this before: Mrs Prasad's lecture on education and responsibility, on character and back-ground, on Character and Background; Chottu's sullen and correct responses. Mrs Prasad speaks the words she must have spoken to her own children, but the words Chottu hears are different. Perhaps it is the way Mrs Prasad sits – on the plush sofa bought by her daughter last winter – and the way Chottu sits, on a stool that you hear occasionally thump the floor in non-verbal remonstrance. Mrs Prasad does not see this difference between how Chottu sits and how her children used to sit. Mrs Prasad means well. She has trained Chottu to sit on stools and chairs, but their relationship is such that Chottu can never sit on the sofa without feeling uncomfortable. Mrs Prasad speaks about Character, something that she and her husband have obviously passed on as a legacy to their own children. Chottu hears about character, something that his parents and their people seem to have been singularly devoid of. Mrs Prasad speaks possibilities; Chottu hears limitations.

The lecture ends and the flat next door fills with painfully pronounced words and sums, with Mrs Prasad's sharp and professional corrections. Chottu is an intelligent young boy, you heard her say to Dr Rai's wife from the ground floor during one of their tea chats, with Chottu bringing in the tea tray, oh yes, a sharp enough boy, but my, is he dense when it comes to reading and writing! He can remember a thousand and one film songs but cannot learn a single poem correctly. Mrs Prasad can only attribute it to lack of 'background'. Background explains much in Mrs Prasad's circles. Background is something that you only get from your family, agrees Dr Rai's wife as Chottu serves them tea and sets down a plate of samosas bought earlier from the halwai around the corner. You feel that right then both of them might even have cast a glance upwards at the Sharmas' flat, for you have heard them attribute the failure of the Sharma daughters to gatecrash into the heavenly realm of the civil service to their 'lack of background'. Mrs Sharma is mousey-looking and illiterate, living in constant dread of the outside world and a particularly malevolent divine providence. Mr Sharma studied in a village and a college in Jehanabad and moved to Patna only when he was posted here. Very few people in the smaller apartments have 'background', though Mrs Prasad and Dr Rai's wife never make them conscious of this serious lack. Not even when they feel that they are faced daily with the envy of people who could have done better but, like Chottu, did not make the necessary effort.

That is what Mrs Prasad sometimes tells Chottu in moments of affection: When you grow up, Chottu, you will envy people like my children the education that you are denying yourself. But Chottu does not envy her children their education. He envies them their ability to return home at will. He envies them their ability to return home bearing gifts.

The flats grow silent. The Sharmas have eaten and Chottu, after being sufficiently educated for an hour or so, has heated up the vegetable curry and made a few chappatis for himself and Mrs Prasad. The TV is switched on in both the flats and discordant sounds filter in from two sides. Provoked by them or perhaps because they have finished studying, one of the six college students who have rented the two-room flat next to the Sharmas puts on Pankaj Udhas. The students don't have a television set. They have an old, black, box-like two-in-one, which functions as a radio until noon and then gets used occasionally as a tinny cassette player in the evening.

The night deepens. You lie in bed. The usual sounds filter in. You lie secure in the precarious knowledge that this is a world that is known to you. Dogs bark in competition from neighbourhood to neighbourhood, the occasional truck rumbles by, someone sings from the embrace of the night – a drunkard or a labourer returning late – doors open and close here and there in the building, the tap in the Sharmas' kitchen drips relentlessly. If it were colder or warmer you would hear the sharp crack of something expanding or contracting in the walls.

The lights go off and someone whoops on the road outside. Then the power cut falls like a blanket of silence. There is a minute or two of deepening silence, finally broken by Mrs Rai's reedy voice. It is not midnight yet and Dr Rai never returns before midnight. One of the two servants is ordered to start the generator and there is the sound of the machine being whipped into life. It catches at the fifth attempt and a low whine fills the building. Downstairs a slight glow rebounds from the facing apartment walls. A bigger, louder generator is lugged into operation somewhere else, but it is so far away that its rough rumble merges with Mrs Rai's sophisticated Japanese whine. The wedding film music that had fallen abruptly silent surges back, louder this time for other competing noises have been stilled by the power cut. The sky grows darker. The occasional howls of dogs are louder and more eerie.

The Sharmas and Mrs Prasad use kerosene lanterns during power cuts, though for different reasons. When Mrs Sharma asks her eldest daughter to light the laalten, she is thinking of the money saved; if she could afford a generator, she would polish it three times a day. Mrs Prasad shouts at Chottu to get the lamps, simply because she has refused to use the Toshiba generator that, like the huge TV and the music system and the car below, was bought for her by one of her children, children whose accomplishments she is otherwise so proud of.

You can imagine the city falling silent, from here through the Gol Ghar and Boring Canal Road to perhaps Gandhi Maidan, so crowded in the daytime and now a place of emptiness and lethargy. But no, you know that the power cut probably does not extend into more fashionable areas. A part of the sky, near the centre of the city, still reflects a diffuse cloud of light.

But this is when the ears start noticing subtle things. A rustle, a silence, a knock. The open window brings in various smells, for this building is not right in the middle of the city. It is not very far from the Ganges, a highway separates these buildings from the river. And the breeze, whose whisper you can hear now, brings in strange, unexpected reminders from the river: that moist fragrance of earth which only people living in dry, monsoon-fed lands can really know and appreciate, the sudden smell of jasmine, the lingering smell of decay, of a rotting body or faeces along the shore of the river. This is not an unpleasant time of the year for power cuts and load shedding, for one does not need fans.

The light surges on, the generators are switched off and you fall asleep. It is a sleep full of sounds. Your father's voice across a decade and three states, the sounds of your past and present, your reality and imagination, all mixed up with creaking beds, footsteps, dog howls, truck sounds, the drip-drip-drip of the tap. You never cease hearing, though you feel that you have heard it all. Once you wake up with the feeling that you have been hearing voices around you, low conspiring voices, that you might even have heard a short shriek; you lie in bed listening and fall asleep again without realizing it.

29 –

The voices of three or four men in the bus raised above the general din. Their accents are rustic, and rusted. A discussion of the problems they had with a neighbouring village over the damming of the water of a stream that flows past both the villages. It had led to two people being injured with grapeshot and a person being thoroughly thrashed with lathis, though not killed, lucky son of a bitch, the lathis bite deeper here than grapeshot, though what respectable village would fire grapeshot in this age of AK-47s, fucking backward rustics, he mutters. They are arguing about the best option this year. Should they fire the first shot this time or should they wait? The matter is evenly poised. Buy a Sten gun, he shouts at them, but they do not hear him, they are too busy haranguing each other, and only the women sitting in the section behind him look up, alarmed.

Sometimes Mangal Singh remembers a trip by an overheard conversation like this one. Sometimes a conversation like this gets italicized in his memory.

30 —

When did I first travel in an Ambassador, wondered Rasmus. Must have been on my first and only visit to India with my parents. How old was I then? Seven years? Eight? Pretty young, anyway. Associated as the Ambassador was with his childhood memories — and faint recollections of an emotionally charged trip — Rasmus felt a kind of irrational irritation at the car. The sort of feeling one has for the black sheep of the family: feelings of irritation, distaste and envy hiding the residue of an unacknowledged affection. So many things have changed in India — even in a provincial town like Gaya — since that trip more than twenty years ago. But the Ambassador still went on. Or at least it did outside the big cities of India, where it was being replaced by Marutis, Fords, Hondas, Mercedes, most of them manufactured in India.

His father had started the trip in the highest of spirits; it had been his first trip to India in eight years or so. His father, never mind Hari's disbelief, had been an Indian. He had changed his surname from 'Sen' to 'Jensen' in Denmark in order to be called for job interviews. Danish names helped in those days. They probably still did, thought Rasmus, though he was too visibly, legibly and audibly Danish to find out from personal experience. He had taken after his mother's family. There was almost nothing of his father in Rasmus, except perhaps in the fact that his hair was dark brown and not one of the shades of yellow that ran in his mother's family, and that ghostly 'mister' that would return to him in unexpected hours.

His father, Dr Alok Sen in India, with a PhD in economics from Delhi University. His father, name finally changed to Alok Jensen in Copenhagen – unemployed, partly employed, finally retiring after only fourteen years of regular employment as a salesman in a firm that marketed windmills and similar technology. His father did not get that job because of his academic qualifications: he spoke seven languages, five of them Asian: the firm had a growing market in Asia.

His father with his ghazals and Rabindra Sangeet that Rasmus grew up detesting. To Rasmus, they were sounds of failure and weakness. He particularly hated ghazals like 'Woh kagaz ki kashti', melodious songs to which his father would sway his head in a kind of nostalgic ecstasy – and then get drunk and embarrassingly emotional later in the evening.

But his father had been different during that trip to India. There had been a lilt to his voice, a spring in his step. He had spoken with such force about Indian food and Indian monuments that even Rasmus – seven or eight years old and with the congenital unconcern of a child of a rich country – even Rasmus had listened. But that was only during the planning stages. The moment the plane landed in India, his father changed again. The crowds, the dishonesty of Indians, the heat, the dust, the pollution, the 'system', the corrupt politicians – these became increasingly his new complaints. It was as if his father's India had been stolen by members of a lesser culture. The people on the streets, the heat, the news – all were considered by his father to be a vicious and premeditated attack on Indian food and Indian monuments, mister. Barbarians, he would mutter, generations of babu sentiment packed into one expressive western word. It became much worse when they reached Ranchi, the town where Alok Sen had grown up and where his parents used to have a large mansion. The mansion had been sold years ago, but it had survived intact in Sen's memory. It had even been replenished in his memory. He was not prepared for the fact that now the mansion was gone, torn down to make way for a complex of smaller houses. He had expected the mansion to be there, housing a family like his own, a family with a family cook with whom Sen would be able to exchange notes. The new houses had housewives or, at best, maidservants who did the cooking.

The barbarians had been there ahead of Sen. They had, in one fell blow, demolished not only the monument of his past but also the entire glorious tradition of Indian cuisine. They had deprived him of the opportunity to get that final elusive recipe from a local bawarchi, that recipe he had sought in vain in glossy cookery books. Rasmus was convinced that it was this disappointment that explained why his parents never went back to India. This and the fact that Rasmus and his mother had spent most of the trip in toilets and retching into copper bowls.

The Ambassador was emitting a series of noises. 'Sassuri,' said Hari, and pulled the car to the side of the road. He switched off the ignition key, cranked the handle that opened the bonnet and got out to take a look at the engine. It appeared to be a minor problem, perhaps the spark plugs, but as Rasmus got out to stretch his legs, making cutting comments about Ambassadors and local mechanics, a thought crossed Hari's mind. A thought or an idea, is how he would later describe it to friends, regaling them with the account, though of course some people might have called it a trick.

They were well out of Gaya but still a few kilometres from the nearest semi-town, Akbarabad. Behind them was a range of barren hills, ahead of them open fields. One large field was full of sunflower plants. The dust of crushed stone coated the few one-storey brick buildings along the roadside.

'Stoncrush Dhabba', said a metal board hanging from the thatched roof of the veranda of the single-storey building nearest to the car. Under the sign, a longer board listed dishes in Hindi. The building, except for the veranda part with its thatched roof over rows of charpoys, was made of brick and had a pukka roof. Half of the pukka part consisted of a kitchen, while the rest was arranged with wooden tables and folding chairs. No one was sitting at the tables though. The drivers and workers preferred to sit on a charpoy with wooden planks in front of them or across their laps to hold the plates and bowls of foods. What would happen to all his firangi theories, thought Hari, if the Ambassador refused to start? Wouldn't they be scattered in the winds like ghasphus? Hari chuckled silently at what he thought was a rather apt play on words. What would happen to the appointment with a state government minister that Ghasmus-sir was so anxious not to miss? Hari toyed with the idea as he fiddled with the engine of the Ambassador.

Then he threw caution to the winds, the slight breeze actually, and took the plunge. Turning to Rasmus he said, 'You very right, sir, Ambassador-sassuri no-good bekaar ki car, sir. It broke now, sir. No easy to repair. Big problem. Take many-many hour, whole day maybe. What to do, sir? No good car, you right, sir. What to do?'

He could see panic creeping into Rasmus's face.

31 ~

A broad ditch covered with water-chestnut plants, their green leaves blanketing the yellowish water. A paddy bird standing still like a statue at the water's edge, its streaked earthy-brown mantle concealing the white feathers underneath and making it merge with the earth, waiting, waiting for a frog to make the slightest mistake.

32 –

You wake late. It is almost nine. You are surprised that you did not hear Mrs Prasad's unmusical bhajan. You hear it every morning, competing with the crows and still somehow imparting a sense of peace to the neighbourhood.

Mrs Prasad's flat is silent, unusually so, but the world is filling up with sounds. The cries of newspaper and vegetable vendors, the bargaining from the landings, the sound of metal buckets being lowered with ropes, buckets containing the money agreed upon and meant to be filled up with the purchase ordered from the vendor below. The students have the radio on; the news is a litany of misfortune and fortune from across the world. Thellas, cars, voices, washing sounds from bathrooms, Mr Sharma performing his elaborate and loud morning ablutions, Mrs Sharma frying puris, old film songs by Mukesh, Rafi, Lata, newer film songs by someone whose name you have never bothered to find out, the sound of an argument from a roadside shop, the cawing of crows: the world sounds exactly as it always has and you eat a slow, safe breakfast. You hear what you have always heard, sounds that are identical but never the same.

You feel you have heard all, but you haven't. You haven't heard the silence in Mrs Prasad's flat. But you will hear about it later. The durban will tell you and everyone else how late last night the three youths were escorted up by Chottu, who claimed that they were village relatives being put up for the night in Mrs Prasad's flat. He will tell you how he should have noticed whether they were carrying bags or not, for he did notice their big bags when they left at the crack of dawn. I ought to have asked Chottu why he needed to escort bigger boys to the train station, the durban would tell you, desperately seeking to be absolved of his share of the blame. But who are you to absolve him, you who heard everything but did not hear enough?

You will hear about the arrival of Mrs Prasad's children, all except the one in Chicago, and the efficient haste with which they organized her cremation. You will hear eyewitness accounts and rumours. You will hear about Chottu for weeks. How he was seen at the station; how he was almost caught in Gaya when he got off the train; how he was last seen (carrying a half-wrapped Banarasi sari and wearing plastic-rimmed sunglasses) where the private Gaya–Phansa buses stopped; how he must be on the way to his village on the Gaya–Phansa route. And then you might hear about what happened to him on a dusty roadway, or he might drop out of the range of all urban hearing. But for the next few weeks the local papers will be full of it, for this is not Delhi. This is Patna, where the walls are still thin.

33 –

The only person in the bus who makes Mangal Singh's restless eyes pause is sitting in one of the front rows. He is dressed in torn but clean clothes, shirt and cotton trousers. He wears thick, black-rimmed glasses. He is obese in a watery sort of way, going bald from both sides of the temple, face swollen in an unhealthy manner. Even from this distance, Mangal Singh can see the dandruff that is spread like powder on the dark cloth covering his shoulders. He seems to be in his own world and it is easy to see that the man is not well. Not well at all. And yet what makes Mangal Singh's eyes stop for a flickering second on the man's face are the signs of gentleness that can be discerned there. Not necessarily breeding or education, but gentleness: the sort of feeling that one associates with a statue of the Buddha, eyes elongated, face serene and loving.

Every once in a while, he spots such men. And sometimes women. He can spot them by the way they hold themselves at a measured distance from everything, connected but not involved. He envies them their distance. Even when they are falling – and this one's clothes indicate a fall of some sort, a steep fall, if he is any judge of the matter, and he can judge falls, he has had more than his fair share – even when they are falling, they seem to do so in slow motion, as if the ground will never really hit them. It is something he has never been able to cultivate. Every time he falls, his hands flail around for handrails to grab. He falls hard.

34 —

And now I could smell Zeenat around the corridor. I had
been paying my neighbours a visit. School was closed for
the winter, leaving me with more free evenings and an
excuse to loiter around a neighbourhood in which most
people knew each other. As it was, I had hardly missed a
single excuse to visit my neighbours since first spotting
Zeenat sunning herself in a faded yellow sari, her arms
bare and bent to comb her long dark hair.

That evening I had seen her going out and had left, as
soon as I could without arousing suspicion, in the hope
of catching a glimpse of her on my way out. I had the
feeling that she had been watching me all evening, while
bringing in the tea and nimkis or taking away the plates.
That was a period of my life when I always had such a
feeling, and not just with Zeenat. I was sixteen, the age of
vague romantic feelings. I had no idea what would happen
if I met her in the corridor or on the stairs. Probably
nothing. I had met her in the corridor or on the stairs a
number of times earlier. Nothing had happened except
her slow and steady wrestling of my gaze to the floor, an

act that took a second or two but felt like a lifetime and left me gasping for breath.

Her smell grew denser. I turned the corner and saw her sitting on the floor at the other end of the corridor, just before the stairs, reclining against the whitewashed, peeling wall. She looked up, caught my eye and wrestled my gaze to the ground. It was all too predictable. But then as I was passing her, my gaze rooted to the ground around my feet, I sensed her feet move slightly. The next moment I was falling, but she had already moved and caught me before I hit the ground. She was smaller than I was – at least a foot shorter – but strong enough to bear my weight and lift me to my feet again. Her arms were round me, her rounded right shoulder supporting me, and she held on for a few seconds more than necessary. Or was it something I fancied? She apologized elaborately for tripping me. My legs slipped, she said.

I hurried down the stairs after assuring her that it did not matter. Her hands were still on me; her smell held me tight as I descended the unlighted stairs. I had reached the bottom when I heard her say, What? I looked back. She stood silhouetted against the mercury lighting at the top of the stairs. Her body – full and firm – was outlined through the sari. What?, she said again, and started descending the stairs. My throat was dry. I mumbled a reply.

I didn't hear you, Irfan babu, she said, coming closer. Now she was just a stair away. Did you say something? she asked.

Trying to keep calm, trying to contain my breathing, I gave the honest answer: no.

No, Irfan babu, she repeated, stepping next to me so that our bodies were touching again, no?

When I put my arms around her and kissed her clumsily, she did not object. Her smell had entered that deep part of my soul from which nothing can ever be erased. It would be there for as long as I lived and, at that moment, I did not care what they said about her. Wanton? Whore? To have her touch me, to feel her firm warmth, I would stand up against all those tongues.

I let my hands wander and touch her breasts. She half led and half pushed me a few metres further, into the doorway of her room. I hardly felt us moving. I did not know if there was anyone looking. Or perhaps I knew that there was no one, for I remember noticing her look around.

Standing in the slanted darkness of her doorway, she pressed closer to me. I grew bolder and cupped her breasts. It was then that I felt her pulling away at the strings of my pyjamas. The act was unexpected. It was too much: it went beyond the bounds of what I had allowed myself to imagine. It brought up echoes of my parents' voices. It brought up an image I had caught from the rooftop and never understood: the old rickshaw puller leaving her room one evening, looking around himself as if he had stolen something.

I tried to pull her hand away with my left hand, the

right one still cupped around a shapely breast. But she laughed, a short, dismissive laugh, considering it a game or a youth's initial reticence, and easily pinning my obstructing arm with one hand, she pulled open my pyjamas and started fondling my penis. Her touch was rough and soft at the same time, it was incredibly lovely and frighteningly knowing. Her smell was as palpable as her touch. You are ready, she said with some surprise.

It was when she let me go in order to squat on the floor and pull up her sari that I gathered together my pyjama strings and fled from the room. The next day I found an excuse to visit cousins in Patna, thinking that distance would take her smell out of my soul. Zeenat left soon afterwards, reportedly because the old aunt spotted her lawyer nephew surreptitiously leaving Zeenat's room one night. She caught a preevaat bus to Phansa, said the ancient rickshaw puller, who appeared to have seen it all, leaving in such a rush that she ran after a departing bus, child in one arm and bundle in another, no aanchal on her head, shouting like the vulgar two-cowrie woman she was. Luckily for her, added the rickshaw puller spitting onto the gravel, luckily for her, the bus stopped.

But that about the lawyer was a rumour I refused to believe.

For weeks after I returned from Patna and learned that Zeenat had left, I would sit on the roof of my parents' house, gazing out into the courtyard of the lawyer. People would cross the courtyard, sometimes the leathery old rickshaw puller in his lungi and shirt, sometimes the lawyer's daughters in shalwar-kameez, sometimes even the bewhiskered aunt in a dress I could not name. But there was no Zeenat sitting in the sun, sari pulled up, legs half bared, her snivelling child playing on the ground. For me the courtyard was desolate now, more than it had ever been, and it never ever filled with the possibility of life again.

You might dismiss it as a teenage crush. But even today when I lie in bed with women who are better looking and more cultured than Zeenat, women who do not need invisible work permits to enter the narrow nation of my love, the reason I inhale their fragrances so reluctantly is that my being is already full of the smell of Zeenat. It is a smell that has never left me.

That, and her short, dismissive laughter filling the corridors of the lost houses of our past.

35

Who was it that had once told him, asleep a face is never the same age as when awake?

Some of the passengers are drowsing. They rest their heads on their arms or the back of the seat in front of them or on the windowpane and sleep fitfully. When they really fall asleep – for five or ten minutes – their faces change. They start looking different. Asleep a face is never the same age as when awake. It looks younger or older, richer or poorer, happier or sadder, lost or found.

When they are jolted awake they sometimes retain the lines of pressure on their faces, creases drawn by the window edge or the seat cover, still half netted in sleep. Mangal Singh notices the pattern of those creases at stops, when he can turn around and survey those he is driving to their different destinations, their many separate stories merging only for those few moments into one narrative of sleep and travel, a novel of travel, he thinks, and laughs, startling the women again and reassuring them this time by putting a finger to one nostril and trying to expel mucus on to the speeding road. This time he is unable to do it with eclat: the mucus drips down the bus side and he is forced to wipe his hand on his towel.

36 ~

Rasmus found himself screaming without realizing it.

'How can this happen? Don't I pay you good mainten-
ance money, mister? What kind of a driver are you? Can't
you repair the bloody junk? This can only happen with
an Indian car and an Indian driver! No sense of time, no
sense of time at all.'

To all of it, Hari responded with abject contrition. He
offered to get a cup of chai from the dhabba for Rasmus,
while he worked, head bowed, body halfway under the
bonnet, on the engine of the Ambassador. Rasmus
shouted a bit more, then he picked up his attaché case
and retired to Stoncrush Dhabba where he bought himself
a lukewarm Coke. He sent the small boy – child labour
as usual, he muttered in Danish – serving in the dhabba
to the Ambassador with a glass of chai for Hari. He might
be in India, but he had not become callous and superior
like Indian employers. He did not eat or drink without
offering his employee something as well.

An hour passed; Rasmus could feel the sunlight getting
sharper, almost on the verge of piercing him through his

coat and crisp cotton shirt. That is how the sun first got to him – as pinpoints of prickly sensation. Hari was still working on the car, head bowed under the bonnet most of the time, imprecations hurled at the car with what Rasmus felt was a rather theatrical tone.

As Rasmus sipped his second Coke, using a paper straw for the first time since childhood – it was typical that they should have paper straws, something he thought had not been manufactured for decades – as he sipped the lukewarm Coke, he heard the clock of his mind striking more and more loudly. Tick-tock-tick-Tock-Tick-TOCK-TICK-TOCK, it went. The attaché case felt heavier too. He could see the road getting more dusty and crowded. There was nothing else to it. He would have to catch some passing bus to Phansa. Hari had been a reliable driver and mechanic in the past, almost a year now, and if he said the car had broken down then it must have broken down. He could not take the risk of waiting for it to be repaired. He could not miss his appointment with the minister. This time, his stay in India had already dragged on longer than anyone had expected; the project had continued to snag on bureaucratic trivialities. He had to keep this appointment with the minister, or he might still be here for the New Year. Dire prospect, that.

He looked down the road. There were a few cars and trucks passing, but he did not think they would give him a lift. Moreover, he was carrying too much money – Rasmus finally had to use the word – he was carrying far too much money in the attaché case to travel outside company. In areas like this, he needed the safety of numbers. He waited. He had waited for about fifteen minutes when he saw it. A bus, gaudily painted, gleaming with metal and tinsel, flowery designs fringing the roof top ... obviously a private bus and not a government one. 'SPEED' and '50 KM' were written on either side of the radiator grille. On the side facing him, Rasmus could see 'PURAB TRAVELS' painted in red, and telephone numbers in smaller letters underneath. Rasmus sprinted to the road, shouting at Hari to repair the stupid car and bring it to the guesthouse in Phansa. He waved; the bus seemed to hesitate and then slowed down and stopped. He knew they would stop to pick him up. They could charge him more.

37 –

At this stop, he turns round 180 degrees and surveys his charges through the pencil-like rods separating his section from the rest of the bus. The bus with its cheap, plastic-covered seats, some torn, the tinsel hanging from the exit and entry doors, the cracked window to the left, the section of women behind him, the firangi holding on to his attaché case, the group of villagers arguing about water rights, the boy carrying a sari with whom Rameshwar is chatting right now, the older men with caste marks on their forehead, the other passengers, mostly male and in their thirties and forties.

This is a ritual with Mangal Singh, this slow sweep of the faces of his passengers for the mind to store, to italicize, to recall this trip by.

38 —

Vilaspur is merely a two-minutes stop on the Gaya–Akbarabad–Phansa route. However, sometimes it takes longer as the Vilaspur bus stop caters not only to local commuters but also to those from fourteen other villages in the vicinity. During the early weeks of summer, after Holi, for instance, when the fields are stubbled and bare and the harvest has been stacked away or sold, there can be quite a crowd waiting for our bus at Vilaspur. That is when the petty farmers and the landless labourers leave the mufassil in search of jobs in Gaya, Phansa or Akbarabad. A crush of ill-clothed men, much darker than me, stinking of sweat and dung-fire, clutching belongings wrapped in dirty gamchhas or old saris. They usually head for Phansa, the biggest town in this part of the state, and end up sleeping on the pavements there. On summer nights, the railway platforms and bus shelters of Phansa are full of these bundled figures. The lucky ones get to pull thellas or rickshaws on a regular basis; the less fortunate go about looking for 'daily' jobs, congregating at the city tower every morning and hoping to be picked by a contractor. Most of these men return to their women and children, whom they leave behind in the villages, when the early monsoon clouds darken the southern sky and the wind carries a moist, warm smell, like that of a shawl worn by a young mother. They return to ploughing their narrow, subdivided strips of fields, or planting and sowing for the richer farmers and benaami landlords.

In the planting and harvesting seasons, they do what they had grown up doing. Farm work. Peasant plodding. That is when they seem to be happiest. I am myself a town dweller – born in Gaya and having worked in Phansa, Hazaribagh, even Patna. I must say I do not share or understand their love for rooting about in the bushes, digging the earth, squabbling over water channels. They talk about it all the time, even when they are on their way to Phansa or coming back. But, of course, the lands are getting narrower and there is less and less profit in agriculture. That is why, every year, some of the men fail to return. They linger on in Phansa, pulling rickshaws, tending private gardens, working on construction sites or as servants and trying to save up enough to put together a jhuggi so that their wives, children or parents may join them. Some drift on to other, bigger places – to Patna, to Kalkutta, even to Dilli. The families of many of these drifters keep waiting in the ancestral village, sometimes forgotten and ignorant of the man's whereabouts, more often subsisting on the meagre money orders he sends. I have seen so many of these

men – the men who board my bus and then return on
it, a little thinner, with deeper lines around the mouth
and the eyes; the men who call their families to join
them, the wife carrying all their bundled-up belongings
and a child, the aged parents bewildered by the prospect
of change; the men who board my old gaadi, a preevaat
bus, and disappear, their wives or daughters coming
down to the bus stop once in a while and standing there
with large eyes. I have seen them all. I have hustled them
in with the cry, 'Private express bus – Gaya–Chaakand–
Bela–Makhdumpur–Tehta–Dhoda–Akbarabad–Janbagh–
Sherpur–Vilaspur–Phansa . . . Gaya–Phansa payn-tees
rupya, payn-tees rupya, payn-tees rupyaaa!' I have sold
them their tickets, gossiped with them, argued, sometimes
even scuffled with those who tried to pay less or travel
free. They are uncouth dehaatis, take it from me, always
trying to pinch a paisa. You have to be careful with them,
even though they might look stupid or illiterate. They are
often stupid, to be honest, but they can be very obstinate
about money. I have ferried all of them to their destinations, clearing their way with the sound of my palms
banging on the metal body of the bus, shouting at carts
and cars to get out of the way. The horn of our trusty
gaadi expired peacefully two years ago – now it gives, at
best, a throaty croak like that of a toad – and the maalik
never bothered to get it repaired. The driver carries a
metal whistle, hanging on a string around his neck. He
blows that when he needs to. I suppose the driver, Mangal

Singh (and before him, Pandey, who did not use even a whistle), could have got the horn repaired or changed. After all, Mangal Singh is a cousin of the maalik or related in some other way – but who hears a horn anyway? Or a whistle, for that matter? You need a khalaasi, a conductor, who hangs out of the door, bangs upon the metal and shouts: 'Get out of the way, watch out, watch out! Are you deaf or what? Arré, you crippled rickshaw!'

That is my job. That is what I do all the sixty-nine *meel* to Phansa and all the sixty-nine *meel* back.

39 –

Distances are relative. He has known that for years now – how one kilometre can stretch for hours or leave a scar in your soul, and how another kilometre can jolt past in a trice, evaporate like a puff of exhaust smoke. In the days when he still read novels – Premchand, Renu, Amritlal Nagar, Nirmal Verma – in those days he used to notice how writers spent pages, chapters even, tracing the narrative across one space and skipped another space with a measured sentence.

But then, he knows, there are distances one measures all through life. He does, anyway. Like Sunita, short of breath now, unable to talk of anything but property and children, like Sunita walking those ten or eleven steps from the kitchen door to hand him a cup of tea. She always brings the tea out to him and asks after his health – she is a stickler for duty and decorum – but he knows that she is not listening to his reply, he could claim to be dead and she would give the same abstracted response of yes, yes, God is kind, for in her mind she is already walking back to

her kitchen of greater concerns, to her domestic order
of belonging.

Some distances are relations, he thinks, and shifts the
gear brutally.

40 ~

The old woman took a pause from narrating her story of the partition. She drank some water from a canteen flask and looked out of the metal-barred window. There were occasional hills and hamlets, toddy trees in the distance and a couple of children defecating down the incline of the railway track running parallel to the road. The whole scene was suffused with a sense of poverty; it covered the trees and the fields like the dust that had settled on the bus. The way she looked at the scene, you would have thought it filled her with some unspoken terror. Perhaps it contained everything that she wished her son and his children would never know, all those memories and fears of deprivation that made her avoid travelling by taxi or buying a car even in her prosperous old age.

But, sister, you seem to be quite well off now, by the mercy of God, said the woman in purdah.

All the women were listening to the old woman's story. Only the young, pony-tailed girl was staring out of the window at the semi-arid fields bumping by, the grey fields that sometimes clenched their fist into a greyish hillock or swelled into a greying village, huts huddled together, an eruption of earth. The sun was stronger now and the bus filling with body odours. It was a warm winter sun, warm enough to cause a dampness under the collar but not warm enough to make you perspire visibly.

That is true, replied the old woman. But that came later. We managed to get the ownership papers to the section of the house we were occupying after seven years. By that time, my husband had got to know the ins and outs of the retail business. We heard of a clothes shop in Phansa that was up for sale. We had been looking for something like that. We could not afford anything in Delhi, but we could afford to buy a shop in a smaller town by then. Though I did not want to leave Delhi and move to a state where there were very few Sindhis or Punjabis, my husband immediately sold off our section of the house in Delhi and bought the shop in Phansa. That is how we came here, sister, and, by the grace of God, we have done well ever since. If you are from Phansa, you might have heard of our shop: Vaishali Suitings and Garments.

That is owned by you, mother!

By my son, now. I am old. Why should I own anything and increase the weight that holds me down to this earth? As the Bhagwad Gita says—

It is a big shop, the woman who had exclaimed said to no one in particular, interrupting even a quotation from the Gita in her excitement. One of the two largest clothes shops in Phansa!

It is the largest, said the old woman, with quick pride. At least, it was when my husband was alive. But Vijay is too young and contented with whatever he gets. Oh, he is a good businessman, my son is, but he does not want to spend more than eight or nine hours in the shop. That is the difference: he did not have to struggle and save. Even when we were poor – except for the first two years – we never denied him anything that he really needed.

Then you must be Mrs Mirchandani, continued the woman who had exclaimed.

Mrs Mirchandani smiled a rather royal assent, while all of us tried to keep our heads from hitting the roof as the bus negotiated a speed breaker with greater abandon than usual. Some passengers shouted at the driver to slow down.

Ahh ... said the woman who had exclaimed, after things – passengers and tempers – had settled down. She had the glazed look that heroines assume in films when they face the hero for the first time or pray to God. Evidently, the Mirchandani name carried some weight in Phansa. Phansa is a small town and being a prosperous businessman there does not imply being a millionaire. But it implies an easy life and the sort of respect that even the marginally rich can inspire in a provincial town.

Tell me this, sister, another woman asked, looking very curious now, is it true that your son is going to marry an Anglo-Indian schoolmasterni?

Oh, you have heard that rumour too, have you? replied

Mrs Mirchandani, without the least surprise or irritation. She stressed 'rumour'.

Vijay is always falling in love with this hair-clipped masterni and that decorum-clipped doctorni. He comes and asks me: Mummyji, I want to marry this woman in skirts or that woman in pants. What do you think? And I tell him, of course you can marry that cheap and ugly woman. With her short hair, she looks like a man, but you can marry her anyway. Only wait until I am dead.

That is the way young men are these days, sister.

No, no, my Vijay is not like that. I know he will never marry someone I disapprove of. And it is not that I want him to marry within the caste. The times have changed and I can accept a girl from another caste, as long as the difference is not too much. I mean, there have to be meeting points. A swan does not marry a crow. She does not have to be a Sindhi or from Sindh or Punjab, but she must be from a good family, maybe a Brahmin, at least a Rajput. And she should be able to make a good wife. Now, if Vijay chooses a pretty, decent woman like this girl here – she pointed at me – I might not object. But he always chooses these cheap, firangi types, with so little hair on their heads and even less sense inside it. Working women, at that.

Mrs Mirchandani turned to me now and asked, But why are you travelling alone, daughter? Doesn't your husband have the sense to escort you? What is your name?

I answered the last question first: my name. I gave the

new name that I had assumed to shake off Iskander Mian. Once Farhana, now Parvati: it hardly mattered to me. These were all aliases that, for one reason or the other, have to obscure my identity, my real name.

Then I explained that I was not married.

All the more reason not to travel alone. You are a decent and pretty girl, you should be careful. In my day, we never travelled alone, no, not even if we went to English schools, said Mrs Mirchandani.

It was then that I saw the opportunity to recruit her to my side. I did not have any long-term plans. I did not expect more than a useful contact or, at the most, help with finding a job in a new place. It was a vague notion, the mere wisp of an idea, but I decided to grasp it. I swear that even as the idea formed in my mind I heard the rasping laughter-cough of our old tabla player and music teacher.

I do not have anyone in the world, mother, I replied, and in a way it was true. I am all alone, a refugee from Kashmir.

Immediately, the old woman forgot the other people in the bus and concentrated on me. The word 'refugee' was enough to arouse her interest and sympathy. She asked me various questions and over the next two stops I spun out a rich story in which my Kashmiri Hindu (Pundit) family was attacked and killed by Islamic fundamentalists. My father, fatally wounded, escaped with me and came to Delhi. He died in Delhi and, since then, I had been wandering about looking for suitable and decent employment. I wept at the end of my story. And I repeated the tale of atrocities that were committed by the Muslims on my family. I could sense the woman in the purdah squirming uneasily at my gory tale, but I had realized that the way to gain Mrs Mirchandani's total sympathy was to bring up the spectre of Islamic cruelty. It appealed to her deepest fears and prejudices, even as my story of deprivation and loss aroused all her sympathy and love. By the time the bus reached congested, dusty Akbarabad I had achieved my end: Mrs Mirchandani had taken me under her ample wings. She had extended a hesitating hand to my shoulder and touched it, something between a pat and a reassuring grasp. Wiping away a tear from the corner of her eyes, she had said, You are not alone any more, daughter. Your mother is with you.

41 -

How, he thinks as he brakes slightly to ease the bus over a rough patch, how relations define distances. How you can stretch out an arm and touch someone, and suddenly, for a second, the hundreds of miles that separate one human being from another dissolve. Like that old woman, the one Shankar has been sucking up to, that old woman touching that girl with the long hair a few stops back. What huge distances such a small gesture can dissolve at times – a small gesture like touching someone's shoulder, or, or, or handing someone a cup of chai with a smile and something other than the usual polite question.

Enough, he tells himself, enough, I have other things to think of. And once again he starts noticing the world, once again he resumes his quest for that image by which he will remember this trip. He can see the small halt of Vilaspur at a distance: it stands out, an eruption of brick buildings on one side of the curving road, with other brick and earth buildings behind it, the large village of Vilaspur petering out slowly into the evenness of the grey and green fields all around.

42 -

Mrs Mirchandani looked like she would say more but at that moment the bus stopped with a jolt, right in the middle of nowhere, and after a few seconds a firangi got on, hugging a dark brown attaché case made of real leather. Everyone turned and looked. He was not the kind of firangi, the hippy kind, who sometimes travel rough on local buses and trains. I have never understood why, but they do. He was the sort that travels only by air-conditioned taxi. For a moment he stood there looking confused, almost on the verge of running out. There was, obviously, no place for him to sit, but then the conductor browbeat a rustic sitting near us into vacating his seat. You are going to get off at the next stop, aren't you, he told the rustic. The firangi hesitated but then took the seat anyway. He placed the attaché case firmly between his feet, knees locked around it, probably afraid of thieves who might run away with it. In a bus like this most people must have looked like latent thieves to him.

It appeared that his car had broken down and he intended to get off at Akbarabad, which was only a few minutes away, and catch a taxi. I guess all of us could have told him that he would not be able to catch a taxi in Akbarabad. There are no taxis in Akbarabad. There are only a few auto-rickshaws, three-wheeled scooters over-loaded with villagers transporting milk in metal canisters and chickens in wire boxes. They sometimes end up over-turning into a ditch without anyone coming to serious harm.

We stopped in Akbarabad next to a line of crowded dhabbas, buzzing with flies even in this season of the year. Electric wires criss-crossed overhead, almost the only sign of Akbarabad being, officially, a town. Auto-rickshaws, tractors, rickshaws, thellas, carts pulled by tired-looking mules, the passing car honking away impatiently, cycles, people, all streamed by the bus. Two roadside sellers – a man and a woman – had spread out plastic sheets by the side of the road and were catering to different kinds of clientele. The man was selling boiled eggs, sliced and garnished with spices, salt and thin slices of onion, and the woman was frying makhana on a small stove and selling it in paper cones.

We stopped for at least fifteen minutes. A beggar tried to get into the bus, but he was shooed away by the conductor and the cleaning boy. This is not a phokat ka gavernmint bus, they shouted at him. Later, the conductor fetched a plate of samosas – two soggy samosas in green chutney – for Mrs Mirchandani. He did not let her pay him back. She shared the samosas with me.

The firangi had spent the time outside the bus, probably looking for a taxi, and when the bus started he was still not back. But then I saw him climbing aboard, looking very dejected, still hugging his attaché case. The conductor had kept his seat for him. He sat down and buried his head in his arms. His collar was already wet with sweat. His coat looked crumpled and dusty, but he kept it on, perhaps because he was wearing a fine light pink shirt underneath. That shirt would not have retained its freshness and colour for more than ten minutes on this bus if it were not covered by the coat.

A boy who had boarded the bus in Gaya – I had noticed him because of the expensive sari he was carrying – that boy had moved to the seat next to the firangi during the stop. He was a pert-looking boy, the sort who would be fascinated by foreigners and babus. Now, gathering up his courage, the boy said a few words in English to the firangi. He spoke by-heart English, the sort of learnt-by-rote lines that even I can muster. But the firangi refused to be drawn into conversation; he shook his head vaguely and stayed silent. He might not have understood the boy, or he might have realized that the boy was not capable of more English than he had already dredged up.

Mrs Mirchandani turned to me and asked, Do you have any education, daughter?

I told her I was a BA. I wasn't but I had gone to school and I could read, write and think for myself, which is more than most BAs.

That is good, she said, girls should be educated. In ancient India, girls used to be educated, she added.

The bus had left Akbarabad after a lot of honking and ringing of bells all around it, and the banging and shouting of the conductor. Now we crossed a narrow and deep nullah of murky water, bubbles floating in it, and were out amid open dry fields once again. The next stop is Janbagh, shouted the conductor. Janbagh–Sherpur–Vilaspur–Phansa. Janbagh–Sherpur–Vilaspur–Phansa.

43 —

At Vilaspur, Mangal Singh gets down to stretch his legs and argue with Shankar. He is still angry with himself for thinking of Sunita, for has he not known more women than he can count, women who did things for him that Sunita cannot even begin to imagine? Has he not lost interest in most women, yes, in Sunita too? And what did Sunita do for him anyway, except hold his hands surreptitiously and peck his cheek in hidden corners? What irritates him – though he does not realize it fully – is not his inability to restore their past in the present, but her ability to erase her past from the present. He feels that something has been killed, something defenceless like an infant. But he doesn't know what. Instead he thinks in familiar terms – he thinks of what Sunita did not do for him and what other women, and men, have done for him. Instead, he works up a resentful anger at himself and gets down to argue with Shankar.

Strange, he thinks, how this cunt of a conductor reminds him of what Sunita has become – all religion, duty and decorum. So that when she comes into the room with the chai now – they are distantly related and she has known him since childhood, so how can she commit the impropriety of sending in a servant? – when she walks into the room for measured seconds and asks a measured question, her decorum so infects him, even him, that he is unable to look into her eyes and recalls each tea trip only by the colour of her bangles, the cup and the pattern of ripples in the cup, superficial images that have to stand in for what he dare not look for any longer.

44 –

I have been plying this route for six years now. The first few years, this bus was driven by Pandey, a hired hand, who was sacked when he pilfered too much petrol from the tank and the maalik caught on. That is when Mangal Singh, a distant cousin of the maalik they say, was brought in. He had been unemployed since his wife ran away, they say; he was – between you and me – a no-good type, an embarrassment to the family. Mangal babu does not pilfer petrol. Instead, he and I have an understanding: we accept the money but do not issue tickets to four or five passengers on every trip. This helps us supplement the ridiculously low wages that the maalik pays us. Yes, he is just as niggardly with Mangal babu as he is with me. The ticket from Gaya to Akbarabad is twenty rupees and the ticket from Akbarabad to Phansa is fifteen rupees. From Vilaspur to Phansa it is seven rupees. After Akbarabad, which is almost a town now, we are not supposed to stop at places other than Janbagh junction, Sherpur and Vilas-pur en route – this is an express bus, after all – but we usually stop for anyone who waves at us, as long as we have space in the bus. Just as we had stopped for the firangi babu five kilometres outside Akbarabad. On a good day, we can make over a hundred rupees on the side during a two-way trip. Driver Mangal Singh and I share the 'take' – except for two rupees that go to the cleaner. These cleaning boys keep changing and usually do not know our arrangement. I think it is a waste to give them any money.

Take this cleaner, a new boy whose name I have not bothered to remember; when I need him I simply shout 'ré' or 'abbé'. On this trip he has kept sneaking away to gossip with one of the passengers, a boy around his age, sitting at the back of the bus and regularly putting on or taking off a pair of cheap sunglasses. I had noticed the boy when he got on at Gaya because he had no luggage, only a Banarasi sari, a very expensive one, half-wrapped in newspaper. Where would a boy of that sort get a sari like that? He must have stolen it from some seth's shop, what else? And our new cleaner has to sneak away to giggle and whisper with that boy with the sari every time I am too busy to pull his ears and set him a task to do. No, I wouldn't share the money with these cleaning boys, all potential thieves, take it from me.

It is also against the sacred precepts of dharm to place temptation and a bad example in the way of children. I myself would not have stolen money in this manner, by Hanuman I swear I wouldn't, if the maalik had paid me decent wages. But Mangal babu insists on the boys being paid a rupee or two. I personally suspect there are deeper, dirty reasons behind Mangal babu's generosity. He is a sensuous man, he lives without a wife, he always hires smart-looking boys – with clean cheeks and tight bodies – and he always makes the boy sit next to him, over the gearbox. I will not say more. It is a sin even to think of such things.

It is in places like Vilaspur that we pick up most of our on-the-side income. In Akbarabad and Phansa people are crafty and may demand a ticket or may even know the maalik. As such, when there is a crowd at Vilaspur the bus stops for well beyond two minutes. It halts as long as it takes the last man, woman or child to get aboard – being a private express bus we do not let people travel on the roof with the luggage.

There was not much of a crowd at Vilaspur today, as is to be expected towards the beginning of winter. Five men, most of whom had boarded the bus at Akbarabad, disembarked, along with the boy with the sari. Two men got in and a woman carrying a tin box and a bundled-up infant. I issued a ticket to one of the men and simply pocketed the other's money. I also issued a ticket to the woman, though she was a thorough dehaati, a dark, snub-nosed tribal woman not even from Vilaspur (where there are no tribals), and I felt tempted not to hand over the counterfoil to her. But then I did. This caused a little argument between Mangal babu and me. He took me outside the bus and berated me for being, in his words, 'a pious fool'. Mangal babu is rather large, flaccid, with folds of flesh around his neck. He wears tiny silver earrings, chews paan all the time, usually has stubble and always has a temper. He has a metal whistle hanging around his neck like a PT instructor. During the summer (and it still gets warm by noon these days), he wears only a lungi and a white banyan when he is driving. Lately, he has been angry with me because I refuse to pocket a greater share of the total ticket money. A couple of months back he had an argument with the maalik – some family matter – and since then he has been complaining even more about the way maalik treats him.

A salary of nine hundred. That is all that skinflint, that housefly-sucking miser, pays his own relation. The mother-fucker! – this has been a constant refrain with Mangal babu lately. Along with that, he has been pressing me to divert 25 per cent of the ticket money into our pockets. I have constantly refused to do so. There is no sense in milking a cow to death. The maalik is no fool. He was himself a bus driver and saved his way into owning a fleet of two buses and five minis. He knows how the system works. He has a pretty good idea of the money one may expect from a bus plying this route. Five or six passengers, around 5 per cent of the total number, may escape unnoticed. Or it may be noticed and condoned: anyone would cheat that much. But 25 per cent? Why take the risk? I am a religious man: there is even a picture of Hanuman on the front panel of the bus, put there by me on my first day, to which I offer a coconut every month. I am not greedy like Mangal babu. I like this job. I make more than what I would doing anything else and I do not want to be kicked out in my middle age. But Mangal babu does not see it that way.

We are slaving away for a fly-sucking skinflint, he keeps telling me. Shankar, you are a goddamn fool if you do not try to take more of the bastard's loot. All the other conductors steal more from the sister-fucker. What are you afraid of? Your Hanuman, He won't mind. There – I have turned the picture around; He won't see you now!

That is the sort of man Driver Mangal Singh is: foul-mouthed and without a shred of piety or religion.

45 -

When Mangal Singh reboards the bus after the argument with Shankar, he feels much better. He looks around at the people he is ferrying to their various destinations. In their faces – sleepy or alert, gossiping or taciturn – in their faces he finds reflected the expressions of all those who have boarded his bus in the past, and for a second – just a second – he allows himself to feel that he has seen it all, that he has seen them all.

46 –

The fields in front of the youth, across the potholed road, were stubbled with what remained of October's crop of ganna, thin yellow stalks jutting out of the powdery brown soil, small birds, sparrows, pigeons, a pair of crested hudhuds, mynahs, squabbling over whatever was still left between the stalks and on the ground. Further on, a few patches of field were being readied for the planting of gehun. From beyond those patches of ploughed-up ground bearing the healing wounds of human intention, from one of the trees beyond the last thin, divisive aari visible to him, came the sound of a koel thinking aloud. O who o who o who shall I hoodwink next time o who o who o whose nest will I lay my eggs in o who o who o who. He was a villager: he knew that this would be one of the last koel songs of the season.

He was a gangly youth of nineteen or twenty, the soft fur of a late moustache only now beginning to show. He wore a terrycot shirt and tight, ill-fitting denim jeans, both torn in a couple of places but mended with skilful rafoo work. Next to him, on the broken brick wall next to the bus stop, there rested a thumbed notebook. There were other people standing at some distance from him. They were evidently waiting for a bus. He was not. You could tell by the way he dangled his feet, the straw that he chewed on. He was probably a college student, you would think. You would be partly wrong: he was still at school. Young men like him had much to take care of at home and took long to finish their school education. If they ever finished it, that is.

Yes, he was simply lazing around. He knew most of the people who lived or worked around this bus stop; his village was only three kilometres away. He was sitting there watching the occasional car or bus pass. He was half hoping that one of those ITDC taxis would come rushing by, taxis rented by rich Indians from big cities or foreign tourists rushing to Nalanda and Rajgir, minor tourist spots that could be done in a day. Usually such taxis would not stop at a bus stand, though sometimes they would stop at really dilapidated villages or a particularly colourful cow or a flock of monkeys, they would stop to spit out two or three tourists, he hoped it would be women, who would click away at the scene with all kinds of cameras. They never clicked at him. Though they did once click at his parents: his father in a dirty dhoti, sporting the right sort of handlebar moustache, and his mother in a sari with a bundle on her head.

He was sitting there on the broken wall, dangling his long thin legs, hoping that one such taxi would stop and provide him a glimpse of women wearing western clothes. He had nothing better to do than wait for such entertainment. His father had harvested their crop last week and, for once, there was no work waiting for him. The cows had to be milked later in the day, but that would be done by his sisters.

He watched the preevaat bus roar into the bus stop. It belched black exhaust fumes, disgorged a few passengers and took on a few. He could recognize the bus by the conductor. He recognized and ranked all buses by their conductors. The conductor of this bus was a religious man with a sharp tongue that he used like a whip against those he disliked and did not fear. Usually the conductor of this bus did not get down at Vilaspur, but this time he got down to confer about something with the driver. They looked angry. Later, when the conductor and the driver returned to the bus, he could hear the conductor shouting at a couple of passengers who had taken advantage of the short stop to stroll away for a pee. The passengers scurried back to the bus, which started with a lurch and a series of bangs. It moved a few metres and then, to his surprise, the bus stopped.

That was actually the only time he felt surprise during the entire episode. Everything else had an aura of inevitability. Even when the policemen came all the way to his father's hut in their village and did not ask about what had really happened, even then he did not feel any surprise.

47 –

But it is not that Mangal Singh sees all of them all the time. He misses things too.

Like he failed to really see the tribal woman until the commotion broke out. He only saw her as money that Shankar let slip into the maalik's coffers.

He did not even see what she was carrying. He saw it and did not see it. Sometimes, seeing is not enough.

48 –

Today Driver Mangal Singh pressed me even more than usual.

Shankar, you pious fool, you will die of starvation, your children will not be able to pay their school fees, your wife will run away with the next-door pickpocket if you do not help yourself to a greater share of that fly-sucking miser's loot. You know how much profit the bastard makes every month? Twenty, thirty thousand. And what do you get? Seven hundred and fifty as salary and perhaps as much on the side? What is fifteen hundred rupees these days? Even a fucking black and white TV costs more!

That may be so, babu, I replied (Mangal Singh is on a basis of economic and social equality with me, but I still address him as 'babu' in deference to his family connection with the maalik. It is things like this that carry you far in life: minor details, like buying samosas for Mirchandani babu's mother). You may be right, babu, but I am a poor man. I am afraid of milking the cow dry.

Mark my words, Shankar, he growled. One day the

bloody cow will kick you in the balls. If you have any, that is.

While we were arguing, a few passengers had come out of the bus, which was rather hot inside as it had not been moving for some time now and the breeze had dropped. Some were stretching their legs, some buying fruits from the only stall (half stacked with bruised bananas, shrivelled oranges, some sweets, plastic combs, glaxo biscuit and cigarette packs, bidi bundles and old magazines), some sipping tea at the two-bench dhabba next to the stall and a couple of men were urinating behind the broken back wall of the bus stop. The tribal woman who had boarded the bus at this stop had been unable to find a seat. As she was so obviously a dehaati tribal – they smell – no one had offered her a seat either. She was standing inside the front door, clutching her bundled-up child as if she was afraid of it being snatched away from her.

Why did you have to issue a ticket to anyone here? Mangal babu demanded again. This was the epicentre of his argument this time. Mangal babu is as avaricious as the maalik. Probably runs in the family – such traits do. He did not want a single Vilaspur passenger to slip away.

These are earth-clod rustics, he kept on telling me. You do not have to fear them. They will never catch you out. Why, that woman there, the tribal, she had probably not even seen a ticket before.

But it is not true that I am afraid. I just do not believe in overdoing a thing. Keep your balance, be content – that is what the scriptures preach. I read the scriptures in Hindi. I listen to the discourse of holy men. Do not push too hard. If you miss a train, let it go; do not run after it. That has been my principle and it has carried me far: from being the 'help' of a motor mechanic, I have worked my way into owning a two-room pukka house. I have a family. I even have a bank account and, if things go well by the grace of Hanuman, I shall buy a minibus within a year and set up on my own. I am a God-fearing man and I retain my balance in all I do. Even the Gita is all about maintaining your balance. I go to the temple every week and I recite the Hanuman Chalisa every morning. But this Driver Mangal Singh, he is different. Rapacious, a womanizer, a drunkard. He has a poster of an actress hanging behind his driver's seat; not a poster of Madhu-bala or Nargis or Hema Malini or even Rekha but of some half-naked two-chit starlet of today. Every time I wipe the picture of Lord Hanuman, he has to say: Why don't you clean the poster of my goddess too? They say he was as bad even before his wife ran away with someone else. Now he frequents the red-light areas in Gaya and Phansa. It is no use arguing with a man like that. So I smiled in a conciliatory manner and reboarded the bus, thwacking my hands on the metal and shouting: All aboard. Hurry up! We are on our way!

49 –

So now, when Mangal Singh finally turns round at the commotion, he already knows what it is about. It is about his inability to see. All the images that are seared into his memory attest to that inability. If only he had been able to see them first, they would not have become indelible. His mind would not have needed to italicize them like a bad writer whose plain words are not sufficient to carry his meanings and stresses.

Behind him, beyond the pencil-like rods separating him from the passengers, people are jostling one another, spilling out of the door. The firangi is clutching his attaché case even harder. And it is only then that Mangal Singh really sees what the tribal woman has been carrying.

But he has just returned to his seat and he does not get out again on hearing the commotion. He remains sitting. Mangal Singh knows with certainty that whatever he does he will remember the trip by this.

Not all memories are voluntary. Sometimes one has no choice but to remember.

50 −

The youth eased himself slightly on the broken wall, as if to let off a fart. The preevaat bus had stopped. It looked like a scuffle was brewing near the driver's end. There were people crowding that end, gesticulating, shouting. He wished they would move for they were blocking his view of a pretty woman sitting next to a fat old woman dressed in an expensive white sari. However, he did not think the trouble was anything worth investigating. Probably a scuffle over a seat.

The conductor of the bus jumped out of the rear door and rushed to the front one. That was probably the fastest way he could get to the spot of contention. Some passengers had also spilled out of the front exit.

That was strange.

He was distracted at that moment by the waddle of a teetar. It was not often that you saw a teetar this close to sites of habitation any longer. It called to his mind an old tune − teetar ké do aage teetar, teetar ké do peechché teetar, aagé teetar, peeché teetar, bolo kitné teetar? − which he started humming as he followed the bird's waddle across the road and into a field. This bird was also different from ordinary teetars, the plump reddish-brown sort that never failed to remind him of some of the middle-class housewives in town. This one was black, mottled and barred with white. It waddled unhurriedly across the stubbled sugarcane field and into a stretch of tamarisk scrub.

The youth had never eaten the meat of a teetar – with increasing prosperity, his parents were slowly turning vegetarian, moving up the caste hierarchy like most Yadav and Kurmi families in the region, though he did not realize it – he had never eaten the meat of a teetar, but he knew that it was considered a delicacy.

Some day, he might set a trap for it in the scrub: he could probably get more for it than for the chickens his sisters and mother reared and, when they were past egg-laying age, sold to the Muslim butcher.

51 ~

From his vantage point high above the crowd that had collected around the steps of the bus, from his driver's seat, Mangal Singh could see more than most.

He could see the men pushing, feeling; he could hear the suspicion and the surprise in their voices. He could feel how everyone, in his or her own way, was already trying to assimilate this thing into the longer and separate stories of their lives, the stories they had brought into the bus and would continue weaving out once they left it, yes, they had no choice but to continue those separate stories – if necessary, stepping over this thing, this unexpected thing, this alien thing that would otherwise make their separate stories redundant.

52 -

The crowd was agitated. It drew the youth's attention away from the teetar. Even some of the women were leaning out of the windows. One woman, carrying a snivelling child, was already out of the bus, jostling in the crowd. Not the pretty woman, though, or the fat old woman next to her. They were still sitting, though he could tell that the younger woman wanted to go out and see what was happening.

The woman with the snivelling child suddenly pushed some of the men away and a space cleared around the front exit of the bus. It was then that he saw the tribal sitting there, hugging a bundle. Was it a thief they had caught? A thief always meant fun. Questions, cuffing, jibes, jokes, threats, beatings. He got off the wall, folded and dropped his notebook into his shirt, dusted his patched, tight jeans, and started walking towards the bus.

53 -

Mangal Singh could see the tribal woman put down the
bundle as if she had nothing to do with it.

54 −

I banged my hand harder on the side of the bus and
the small bus stop rang with the sound of flesh on
metal.

Mangal Singh had already gone round to the other side
and pulled himself up into the driver's seat, probably
swearing at me under his breath. I saw him joke with the
cleaning boy: he always has a friendly, unprofessional
relationship with these boys, which makes them lazy, and
cheeky with me. He started the bus.

Hurry up! Hurry up, you two! I shouted to the men
urinating behind the broken wall. One of them hurriedly
wrapped up his dhoti and ran to the bus. The other −
from a big town by the look of the stiff collar of his
checked shirt, his shiny terrycot bell-bottoms, his thin,
trimmed moustache and his Brylcreemed hair − took his
time. Hurry, hurry! I shouted, the Green Revolution has
been long over!, and hanging out from the back door, I
again banged upon the metal.

What is the hurry? said the young man, stroking his
pencil-thin moustache as he finally sauntered up and

brushed past me into the bus. He had a scar on his left cheek and probably considered himself a tough guy. We are not catching a plane, he scoffed.

He took out a red plastic comb from his pocket and combed his hair.

Finally, all of them were aboard. I banged thrice on the side to signal to Mangal babu to start driving, but for once he did not need to be prompted: the bus was already crawling out of the stop. Just then there was a commotion near the front door. I could make out a man's voice over the general uproar. He was saying – The child is dead. I am telling you, the child is dead! Touch his arms, they are cold, thanda like ice.

More voices pitched in, expressing surprise, indignation, shock, scepticism, anger, plain curiosity.

The bus started slowing down.

I jumped out of the rear exit and ran to the front. A crowd had already spilled out, while a bigger crowd was hanging around the front exit and peering from the windows on our side. On the bottom step of the door sat the tribal woman. She was clutching the bundled-up child to her bosom.

The child is dead. She is carrying a dead child, cried the dominant male voice.

The woman shook her head, absent-mindedly, while still clutching the child. Some of the men tried to feel the child. It could not have been more than a couple of months old.

He is right, the men who had felt around in the bundle cried. The child is not alive. It is cold.

It is not breathing!

It is cold like ice! No life.

The terrycot-bell-bottoms-Brylcreemed townsman, who had taken his time urinating, shouldered his way to the squatting woman. He felt the child. He exuded the false authority of someone who just had to know everything.

Your child is dead, he told the woman, in a measured, matter-of-fact tone. Why are you carrying a corpse into the bus?

Not dead, said the woman, emotionless and unmoving.

It has been dead for hours, insisted the Brylcreemed townsman. It is ice cold.

He is only ill, replied the woman. I am taking him to his father in Phansa. There are doctors in Phansa.

Where does your husband live?

In Phansa.

Where in Phansa?

I do not know. He went away five months ago. He went to Phansa.

Another of the ones who disappear, I thought.

How can you take him to his father when you do not even know—

Anyway, I broke in, having had the time to examine the corpse. The child is dead. There is no use taking it anywhere.

That is right, muttered a few voices. There is no use taking it anywhere. It is dead.

It took us fifteen minutes or more just to convince the woman that her child was stone dead. These rural women are so obstinate in their ignorance. That is why when I married I looked for a girl who had been born and brought up in Phansa – not in a huge debauched city like Kalkutta or Dilli, but not in a village either. We turned the child over, uncovered the body, made the woman feel the coldness there and the lack of heart beats, even pointed out the faint stench of decay that had started emanating from the corpse. Finally, she stopped saying 'not dead'. But she did not weep or go away. She placed the child on the ground before her feet, as if the child no longer belonged to her, and remained sitting on the steps.

55 –

And then Mangal Singh saw it, the image that would stay in his mind, that would fill up so much space in his imagination that the rest of the trip would be washed away from his memory. His mind, greedy author, italicized it on the pages of his memory even though he, for one, could never tell that story. Not really. Not fully.

56 –

Before the men started shouting excitedly – and it took Rasmus a few minutes to understand what they were saying, so different were the dialects of most of them from any kind of Hindi he had heard till then – before the shouts broke into his silent calculations of time and duty, Rasmus had already been vaguely conscious of the many strands of voices that filled the bus with a low hum. The many conversations that wound into one another and then separated. He thought later that they were like the tilkut he had seen being twisted and kneaded around wooden posts with short handles in Gaya. The strands of tilkut snaked around the post, merged and separated, separated and merged.

But now suddenly there was only one reality of conversation on the bus. Death. But it was not at all the kind of death Rasmus could recognize. It did not have the ordered decorum, the regulated heaviness, the dutiful attendance of the deaths he had witnessed or heard of in Denmark. It did not separate itself clearly from life. The strands of this death remained intertwined –

horrifically so for Rasmus – with life on and around the bus.

People were moving to the front of the bus, jostling each other, craning their necks to get a better view. Rasmus tightened his grip on the attaché case.

57 –

What Mangal Singh would remember most vividly about this trip were the two flies probing the concavities of the child's nostrils, impervious to the seething of life around them, impervious to the silence of death that sat like a blush on the child's face.

58 ~

When the village youth walked up to the bus, half the passengers were already out. Only three or four older men – caste marks on their forehead – were still in the bus. And most of the women.

The woman with the snivelling child – quite an attractive woman, he thought, but cheap-looking, without an aanchal on her head – was still pushing the men away, shouting, Give her some space, let her breathe!

He was disappointed. Maybe it was not even a thief. It sounded like someone had just fainted. But then he heard the voices more clearly: It is dead; the child is dead. Just then the crowd at the bus door parted to allow a firangi to get off, a tall man who looked very much out of place in the bus, and the youth caught a glimpse of the dead child in the tribal woman's arms.

She was sitting on the front steps of the bus.

Her arms were tattooed with abstract designs.

She was the only spot of stillness and silence in that seething mass.

59 –

Finally, it was simple: *Two flies probing the concavities of a dead child's nostrils.*

60 ~

Take the body back to your village, I told the tribal woman, who was slowly, wordlessly rocking on her haunches now. Take him home; the elders will know what to do.

I repeated myself when she did not reply.

There is no one there, she said.

No one? I snapped, a little angry with this woman, her tribal thickheadedness. No uncle, no grandmother, no father-in-law?

No one, she repeated.

But don't you see, woman? You cannot go to Phansa with a dead child. There is no use.

I did not want us to be delayed further. We still had to make our return trip and neither is this road fit to be used after dark nor is the region as safe as it seems to be in daylight. There are criminal gangs operating from almost all the villages, criminals and communists. I was also afraid of a police enquiry and related problems. It is best to steer clear of policemen and the law.

She sat silent. Dense as amavas night.

We should help her cremate the child, said the Bryl-creemed bigtownsman, stroking his thin moustache thoughtfully. He was the sort who had to have all the answers. He seemed to puff up at the importance of his own suggestion, so that his ribs stood out under his tight checked shirt.

The tribals of this area do not cremate the young. They bury them, I broke in sharply, trying to dismiss this crazy, time-consuming idea of the town-babu. No one listened to me. At that moment the firangi, who surprisingly knew some Hindi, broke in and told us in broken Hindi that the police should be called. Police bullana, police bullana, he repeated. Rule sé kaam karna, certificate karna, he said. No one paid any attention to him either.

Then let us help bury the child, the townsman was saying, and the rustics were listening to him. Not to me, not to the firangi babu; they were listening to that self-important city-slicker with a thin moustache and Bryl-creemed hair!

We will bury your child, he told the woman.

Yes, yes, we will help you bury the child – chorused a few other voices, most of them dripping with rustic sounds and the sentimentality of villagers who would not, on other occasions, hesitate to beat a person to death for diverting a water channel.

The woman remained impassive. The townsman officiously beckoned a rustic lad to pick up the body and led a procession outside the bus stop and down a flank of the road into the thin strip of government land separating the road from the fields. Only some of the better-dressed men, from some mufassil town or the other, and a couple of older villagers with caste marks on their foreheads stayed away from the body. Mrs Mirchandani, of course, stayed where she was; so did the respectable woman sitting next to her. The small procession stumbled down the flanks of the road. This strip of government land was covered with dry grass and straggly bushes. Here and there were spots where the government had tried to plant trees, hedged in by a few bricks and strands of wire, but most of the trees had died or been stripped bare by goats and cows.

Where is a shovel? Does anyone have a shovel? cried the bigtownsman. After a moment of confusion, one of the locals – a youth whom I had seen sitting on a broken wall and watching the tamasha – ran off to a room behind the dhabba and returned with a shovel. The Brylcreemed townsman beckoned another rustic-looking man to commence digging. He was obviously the sort of man who just had to be in control, full of his own importance. A shallow pit was dug, the child's body placed in it and covered up. We marked the spot with some bricks from the broken wall of the bus stop and the hedges that the government had put up for non-existent trees.

The tribal woman was still sitting on the steps when we returned. She had stayed there throughout. So had the firangi, muttering something about law and order, police and regulation. I knew how he felt. I too have felt like that with these irrational rustics. The brazen-looking, cheap woman who had jumped out of the bus with a snotty child in her arms had also stayed with the tribal, sitting on the same step, touching her on the head, theatrically stroking her matted and snaky hair. Her own child was toddling around on the ground, trying to pry something out with a stick, apparently unattended.

We have done it, I said, wanting the tribal woman to move and let us continue with the journey. We were already late by two hours or more. There is no need for you to go to Phansa now, I added.

She got up slowly. The cheap woman with the snotty child handed her the tin box that the tribal woman had been carrying. The tribal started walking away.

Wait a second.

This was again the officious bigtownsman: You have not refunded her ticket money!

Yes, yes, came the voices again, the same sentimental chorus: You should refund her money. Yes, yes, you should.

This placed me in a tight spot. I had issued her a proper ticket, torn it out of the book, and there was no way I could convince the maalik that the ticket had been refunded. We even had a placard saying 'No Refunds' in red, just behind the driver's section. If I refunded the money, I would have to make up for it out of my own pocket. And I am a poor man, with a wife and two children.

I cannot refund the money. I have already issued the ticket.

This sparked a heated debate. The woman kept standing there, probably unable to push her way out of the crowd that surrounded us, while the townsman grew more and more belligerent on her behalf.

I turned to Mangal babu for support. He had remained in the driver's seat all through the episode, placidly chewing a paan, fanning himself with a dirty towel and following it all from a distance. He is not like you or me, not at all the sort of person who puts himself out for others.

Ask the driver sahab! I shouted. He knows I cannot refund the money even if I want to. It is not my money. Not even if my own mother died.

You will have to, you will have to, even if it is out of your own pocket, screamed the townsman, puffing up so much that his ribs, which were quite visible now, take it from me, would have burst out of his chest. You will have to, you cannot exploit the poor, the days of the Laatsahabs with their khansamahs and ardallis are over, you will have to refund her ticket even if it is from your own pocket, he shouted.

Oh, yes, I shot back. Why don't you do it then?

But I could feel the situation turning nasty. 'Exploiting the poor' was a well-formulated phrase, a clever one, and the Brylcreemed townsman knew that.

I turned back to Mangal babu, addressing him through the open front door. The firangi had already returned to his seat, clutching his attaché case. He had also taken off his coat, finally.

Tell them, Mangal babu, I pleaded. Tell them it is not possible for me to refund the money once the ticket has been torn out. I have to account for every naya paisa!

Instead, Mangal babu dipped into his underwear-lining and brought out some rolled-up one- and two-rupee notes. He handed them to me without counting and said slowly, Give it to her.

I took his money after a second's silence all around. Even the Brylcreemed townsman had not expected this: it took the wind out of his sails. The ship of his social-ist eloquence floundered. His ribs disappeared into his checked shirt.

The ticket cost only seven rupees, I said, counting out the rupees and handing them to the impassive tribal woman. The jeans-clad youth who had fetched the shovel broke into moronic impertinent giggles, but I stared him into silence.

The rest of the money I returned to Mangal babu.

61 −

Where else but in India? Where else but in India?

Rasmus could hear his father, Alok Sen, alias A. Jensen, utter that sentence. His father had said it in two different ways. In Copenhagen it had been a statement of pride: Where else but in India you have eighteen, eight-teeeen major languages being spoken side by side? Where else but in India you have so much history? Where else but in India could independence be achieved by non-violent means? Ahimsa, ahimsa, his father would repeat, drawing out the word. Know what it mean, mister?

But as soon as Alok Sen alias A. Jensen landed in Delhi, the burden of the phrase had changed. The stress had moved to the second half of the sentence: Where else but in India does one have so much bureaucracy and inefficiency? Where else but in India can one see such poverty? Disgusting! Criminal! Simply criminal! he would expostulate.

And now, bumping along on the potholed road, trying to keep his shirt from getting too dirty, Rasmus spoke to his father in his mind: Where else but in India could a bus stop to bury a child and then proceed as if nothing has happened? Nothing much anyway, it seemed to him, for he could hear some people discussing what had happened and the young woman who had handed the aborigine her box was now cuddling her child with an excess of emotion.

Where else but in your India, Rasmus asked his dead father. Where else but in bloody India?

Mister.

62 –

It had been a long journey, longer than usual. But we are finally at the corner near Phansa chowk, where the private buses stop. The corner is congested with private buses, coloured, glittering metal, resin seats with the stuffing pulled out, gods and saints and lines from the Qur'an hanging in the driver's cabin, videos and music systems blaring. The chowk is teeming with people. There are people in a rush to catch a bus or a rickshaw. There are vendors. Chinniabadaam, chinniabadaam, chinniabadaam, calls the roasted-peanuts vendor. There are women in purdahs, women in saris and women in shalwar-kameez, one of them even without an aanchal. There are men with gathris and men with suitcases. There are children. A bus starts with a roar. And the other conductors are shouting.

I have had trouble with Driver Mangal Singh again. He wants the stop to be of the usual two hours. But we are already two hours late and I want to get back to Gaya before it gets dark. The day has been inauspicious enough. A dead child. One should not even think of such things.

I would have left in fifteen minutes, but Mangal Singh

has to perform the only act of worship he knows: eating, stuffing himself. So we will be leaving in one hour. I slap the cleaning boy lightly on the head and tell him to hurry up. Don't sweep the rubbish and the vomit under the seats, clean it properly. I want to see your face reflected on the floor, I say to him. Then I retire for a cup of chai at Nizami Restaurant. I always carry my own food. In a few minutes I will start banging the bus again, shouting my chant in reverse: 'Private express bus – Phansa–Vilaspur–Sherpur–Janbagh–Akbarabad–Dhoda–Tehta–Makhdumpur–Bela–Chaakand–Gaya . . ., Phansa–Gaya payn-tees rupya, payn-tees rupya, payn-tees rupyaaa!'

Another journey, other homes. I think of the bus I will buy if things keep going well. My own bus. I have to keep thinking of the bus I will buy. I cannot afford to be distracted by the farce of life all around me, the tragedies and comedies of people who have lost sight of their destinations.

63 –

When Rasmus got to the guesthouse, after having met the minister directly off the bus and in a confused state of mind, Hari was already there with the Ambassador. 'Ghasmus-sir, Ghasmus-sir, what happen, sir, bus come very late, sir?' he asked Rasmus with an excess of concern.

The guesthouse, with its ravaged lawn and few flowers, its cool, heavy-beamed bungalow, the guesthouse felt like paradise to Rasmus. It almost made him forget his irritation at Hari.

Rasmus was particularly irritated by the fact that Hari had repaired the car and managed to reach Phansa not much after the bus got there. He knew that it ought to have made him appreciate Hari's skills as a mechanic, for he had cast serious aspersions on those skills before catching the bus, but it merely irritated him further. Had the Ambassador really been in such a bad condition? The thought crossed Rasmus's mind that perhaps Hari had put him to all this trouble – not to mention the nightmare of the dead child's burial – from negligence or malice.

But then he looked at Hari, noticed the man's almost

comical desire to please, and he dismissed the thought. Rasmus was also feeling happier, lighter – the attaché case that he had left with the minister's private secretary had lifted a burden from his soul. He had done what he had to do. Where else but in India, he thought, then he shrugged his shoulders and entered the guesthouse to freshen up and eat before the return trip. They might as well get back today.

64 –

That evening the youth returned late, much after his sisters had finished milking the cows. He had the daal-chawal that his mother had left on a thali covered with a pattal in the corner of the smaller room that served as a kitchen and the bedroom of his mother and sisters. He took care not to wake them up. Then he returned to the outer, the bigger, room which served as a baithak during the day and a bedroom for the men at night. His father was sleeping on the only charpoy in the house, snoring intermittently, though he woke up and said, 'You are home?' before turning round and resuming his intermittent snoring.

The rooms were filled with the smell of cattle in the adjoining shed. The banked smell of four cows, three goats and a wire-net coop containing seven hens and a rooster. A good herd by village standards. The buffalo was tied outside the shed. It did not need to be shielded from dew or the unexpected shower.

At the entrance of the shed was a stuffed calf, leaning against the mud wall. The calf had died soon after birth.

It had been stuffed and the stiff brown effigy was carted to the mother twice a day so that she could lick it with her powerful tongue and continue to give more milk than usual.

No one had ever laughed at that cow.

He had felt like laughing for hours after the bus left. Laughing, but not from happiness or ridicule. He could not fathom the wells of this desire to laugh.

He lay down on the covered straw bed on the floor, next to his two brothers and the cousin who lived with them because his uncle had five other sons and less land. He felt very tired, but he did not sleep until the sky started growing lighter and he could hear a growing rustle in the hen coop made of wire and wood in the shed attached to their semi-pukka house. Soon the rooster would crow. Once, twice, thrice.

65 –

Everything else followed naturally, though I had not planned it out on the bus. Far from it. What happened with the tribal woman continued to haunt me all the way to Phansa, though Mrs Mirchandani was determined – perhaps for my sake, for she thought that I was still recovering from the loss of my family – Mrs Mirchandani was determined to talk about other things. She was also a woman who could not really sympathize with the losses of those who were too dissimilar, and, to be honest, most of us are like that. She spoke about various things, while the tribal woman stalked my mind and thoughts. No, I did not have the time to think of the future in the bus. And if I did, all I wished for was a shelter over my head and a job.

But things took a turn of their own, as the tabla master would have said, laughing and coughing.

Vijay Mirchandani turned out to be more or less as I had pictured him: an easy-going, mildly religious man in his early forties, with a pleasant face, skin a bit rough and swarthy, an underexercised body, and an unfed hunger for a woman. A few days were enough to make him forget his Anglo-Indian teacher – who was probably a friend rather than a lover – and start paying attention to me. It would take me longer to forget the tribal woman.

Once I realized what was happening, I went about it in a demure way. I never, not even once, made him feel that I was taking the initiative now. I made tea for him and laughed demurely at all his jokes. I accidentally brushed against him, and blushed. I looked at him and, when he glanced my way, I looked away suddenly. If Mrs Mirchandani noticed what was going on, she ignored it. Perhaps she could not imagine her son contemplating anything of a permanent nature with a penniless orphan. Moreover, she was happy to get the gossip-maligned Anglo-Indian teacher out of circulation and she genuinely liked me. Once when I was massaging her feet, she stroked me on the head and said: If you were Sindhi, I would marry you to Vijay. You are so well behaved and you have our culture in every vein and cell of your body. It is so rare to meet women like you these days, daughter. May you live long.

I did not tell her that many of the nuances of 'our culture' that she so appreciated in me had been learnt under a Muslim ustad and were part of the culture of the very people whom she would never forgive. If she wanted to have nothing in common between those people and her own, she would have to marry off her son to the sort of tribal woman who had boarded the bus that day. And even then she might not succeed, for human beings are like pieces of cloth in the rain of time: porous. Cultures seep into us; we get heavy with our and everyone else's history. I could tell her that, but I would not.

Then one evening, when Mrs Mirchandani was away at one of her frequent kirtans or religious darshans, Vijay came home early. He walked over to me. I was in the kitchen, cooking the dinner.

Cooking foo-foo-food? he asked, gulping hard.

I adjusted my sari's pallu so as to cover my head and hide part of my face. It was a gesture expected from any decent girl in the olden days.

Why do you cover your face all the time? said Vijay, gulping harder. You have such a nice face. You should not keep it half hidden.

Don't say things like that, I murmured, sounding flustered.

Why not?

Just don't.

Why not?

You know.

Why not? he repeated. My pretended confusion had had the right effect on him: he was growing bolder and had stopped gulping like a rehu fish.

It is not right, I said.

It is not right? What is wrong about telling a woman that she has a beautiful face?

After a second he added, in a low, hoarse voice: And a body like chandan.

With that Vijay moved closer, so that his body touched mine. I shrank away, but not too far. He followed me and put a tentative arm around my waist. I let him do so. But when he raised my face to kiss me, he found tears trickling down my eyes. Luckily, I had been frying onions only a few seconds back, and the tears looked natural. Vijay grew apprehensive. He stepped back and asked, What is wrong? Don't you like me touching you?

What does it matter, babu?

Of course, it matters! I am not a monster!

You are the master of this house and I am a homeless orphan, a servant, a slave. What does it matter what I feel?

Is that what you think? said Vijay, looking relieved. Do you think I am merely fooling around with you?

I am too helpless to think, babu.

I am not playing around with you. I have been watching you for weeks. I am in love with you, declared Vijay.

It is only the rich who fall in love, babu. What can I say? If I object, you will throw me out now. If I do not object, you will throw me out later . . . when you fall out of love. I will lose the only thing I have left in my life: my . . .

Vijay looked taken aback at these words. Then he said: What if I married you?

Your mother will not agree to it, I replied.

She will.

No, I will not let you do something that will hurt your mother. She is my master. She is my god.

66 –

Later when the police officer came to interrogate him, he maintained an idiotic, half-comprehending silence. His father was sitting next to him, squatting on the floor like him before the officer. The officer was sitting, cross-legged, feet pulled up, on the charpoy that had been dragged out for his convenience. Two constables stood stiffly next to the charpoy. His mother stood behind the officer and the constables at the low doorway of their semi-pukka house, his sisters crowding big-eyed behind her.

He had thought they would ask him about that mound of earth and rubble by the roadside. He had thought they would ask him about the baby they had buried. But they were not interested in that. They were looking for a boy called Chottu who had killed someone in Patna, one Srimati Prasad, and run away with a lot of money and jewellery. The boy lived in one of the neighbouring villages, said the officer.

He could tell that for the officer all the villages in the area were copies of the same undeveloped prototype. They did not exist, like they did for him and his family, as distinctive entities, one known for its crop of mangoes, the other for a particular sweet, one famous for the short temper of its inhabitants, the other for the generosity of the villagers.

No, he replied, no, he did not know anyone from that village.

No, he did not know anyone called Chottu.

He came from a long line of peasants who believed in not telling policemen anything unless they were sure that it was exactly what the policemen wanted to hear. He did not mention the boy he had seen sneaking away as they buried the baby. The boy carrying what appeared to be a single resplendent Banarasi sari. He did not say anything about that boy, though he heard later that they caught Chottu anyway. When he had last seen him, Chottu was cutting across the fields, walking with practised ease on the aaris. The way he walked showed that he was not unfamiliar with the narrow ridges and pathways of rural life. On any other day, he would have paid more attention to someone getting off at the stop and walking in the direction of his village and the villages around it. But he had been busy fetching a spade at that time and his last memory of Chottu, for who else could it have been, was that of a boy like he himself was a few years ago, a boy in shorts walking fast on the narrow aaris, sunlight glinting off the rich material of the Banarasi sari that he carried under one arm. When he looked for the boy again, after the baby had been buried, there was no sign of him. Distance had swallowed him up. Though he fancied seeing something glinting a long way off.

67 -

The telegram from the Delhi office that Rasmus received a few days later made him buy a bottle of whisky to celebrate with the Danish tourist he had met in Bodh-Gaya and the Indian manager of the Gaya office. It meant that his extended – almost year-long – deputation in India could be wound up in a few days. The joy of the telegram made him forget the irritation with which he had carried the attaché case to the minister's residence. He even forgot the dead child and remembered it only later, in Copenhagen, as an instance of the extremities of India. The many strands that go into the making of tilkut, the twisting and turning, the grunting and wrenching, the merging and separating, all that would be invisible in the finished and cooked tilkut of narration that Rasmus would feed his audience in Copenhagen. Why don't you write a novel on it, his girlfriend would say, something dark and sinister, heavy and Kafkaesque, or something light and irreverent, funny and magic realist like that whatsisname Rushdie writes?

The telegram said: CONGRATULATIONS STOP IDEA

GIFT TRIP WORKED STOP ORDER IN HAND STOP ALLA
SIR TAK STOP

The last sentence, Rasmus guessed, was a corruption of
'alle siger tak'.

68 –

Vijay went away baffled. But he was back very soon.

That evening, the next day and every day for three weeks afterwards, I encouraged him with words and accidental touches, and put him off at the last moment. I could feel him getting desperate. He forgot to shave. His well-oiled hair started looking awry. The moment his mother went out, he dropped in and hung around me. And then one evening, while Mrs Mirchandani was away at another kirtan, he burst in and grabbed my clothes. I tried to protest, but he started kissing me, whispering, I will marry you, I will marry you, I promise I will marry you.

Promise, promise, promise, he repeated, like a child offering a solemn and only half-understood promise to another child. But his voice was not that of a child; it was congested and hoarse.

Vijay is not very strong – I could have pushed him away if I had wished to. But while I continued to protest, I let him have his way with me. The way he did it, I could tell that he had never been to bed with a woman –

in spite of all that talk about the Anglo-Indian teacher. No wonder: with a dominating mother like that and all her high, religious expectations! I had to help him do what he wanted, while pretending to resist him all the time. He did not see the difference. None of the differences. At the end of it, I just sat and wept. Pathetically. Abjectly. Unconsolably.

I knew that his conscience would do the rest of my work. I stayed in my room the next day, feigning a headache when Mrs Mirchandani enquired.

A day more, and it was done. He fixed up a local pujari and got married to me without a word to his mother. Then he told her. Baap ré, did the old woman shriek! She tore her hair, she beat her breast, she threatened to leave her son's house. For a moment I thought that all my efforts at pleasing her in the past had been wasted. But by the next morning, she was merely sulking. A week later, she spoke to me for the first time since the disclosure. Within a month, she had accepted our marriage – on the condition that we get married again with extensive rituals and under her supervision.

Come, daughter, she said to me, I always liked you and perhaps it is for the best. After all, you are my daughter and a Kashmiri pundit. You will make a perfect wife. Let's forgive and forget.

Forget. Yes, maaji, that is what I want to do. Forget. Forget who I was. Forget Chaand. Forget the rasping laughter-cough of the tabla master slowly bleeding to death. Forget the look – or the lack of any recognizable look – on the tribal woman's face. Forget and become respectable. Yes, maaji, I will forget. I will be good at forgetting.

But of course I did not say all that. I knew that in my new life there would be many things I would never say. I only bowed my head when she repeated: You were already my daughter. You will be the perfect wife.

And that is what I am now. There was a time when I could have been the keeper of the harem keys, a guard of the holiest of holy shrines in the Middle East, a dancer, a soldier, a spy, a scholar, a general in Delhi. I am not any of these today. But, then, I am something that is even harder to achieve for so many. I am the perfect wife.

I am not Farhana Begum or Parvati any more.

I am Mrs Mirchandani.

I will not be buried by strangers at a roadside. My fate will be another story . . . no, not that one.

69 -

The night that envelops his village is a deep one. In its darkness you can see the stars. The stars are brighter out there than in towns and cities.

There are no stars on the land. If there had been daylight, you might have seen the neighbouring villages. But at night the villages light no lamp beyond the waking hours. Unlike the sky, the land wears its night without the cover of stars.

He is not laughing any longer. He is sleeping. Fitfully, like a bus passenger.

Homes, Again

There, the bus has stopped for the night; we have all returned home.

Home.

A word that, in English or Danish, is spoken with a final clamping down of the lips, like windows shutting, as if what was contained was nothing but space; there is a movement like that of a possessive child gathering his toys in his arms: home; and that, in Hindi or Urdu, is spoken with a soft expulsion of breath, the lips opening like doors, a moving out from the rasp that catches in the throat to the final roll of the tongue: ghar.

Ghar is also house.

We have all returned home, or at least to houses. I have the home of my memories, that house of, shall we say, sixty-nine rooms. It is through the windows of those helter-skelter rooms that I first saw the world I have tried to show you, those rooms that are all jumbled up – as if in a bhoolbhoolaiya, as if in a house added to and demolished over the years, as if in one of those mental states (like dreaming or remembering or meditating) when there is a seamlessness in the way things flow backwards and forwards. My homes – fragile, confusing, monstrous – have not been contained by Ammi ké yahan and Ghar, even though I have always borne their burden.

Parvati, Farhana, whatever her name is, has found a home too; she has found a respectable home, the house of the Mirchandanis, the house of suiting and shirting, the house of readymade garments. Hari has returned, at least for this night, to his wife whom he won't scold tonight, no, far from it. Rasmus is back in Gaya and will soon be returning to his girlfriend in Hillerød, to their three-room flat in a nineteenth-century building, to the candles that they light every evening, the framed paintings, the potted plants, the dusted order of belonging. Wazir Mian is in the house he built over the years, the contentious house of his sons. I wish him an old age free from litigation. I wish him fields not subdivided into plots. I wish him only mild squabbles over water channels. And his son, the one with the pencil-thin moustache and Brylcreemed hair, the one with the livid scar, he is there too, in that house he resents because it is in a village and he would much rather live in a town. You, you are in your flat in Patna, TV on, sound switched off, waiting for the tap-sigh-tap of Mr Sharma's tired steps. The boy who would end up being lonely in large cities where women smell good, the teenager once in love with brazen Zeenat still has a home, and surely Zeenat and her snotty child will find another house to work in. They always do. The conductor, oh yes, the conductor, we know he has a home, a house he has built with much labour and effort and planning, a house with the large framed painting of Lord Hanuman, garlanded, with an agarbatti smouldering near it; and Driver Mangal Singh has his kamra too into which walk, sometimes, garishly painted women, women who wear scarlet lipstick. Even the village youth who sat on the wall and fetched the spade has a home. I am not a magician; I cannot really take you into the semi-pukka home of that youth, but I can point it out to you if you slow down a little. There, there it is, next to the peepul tree, hunching into the rest of the village, a ploughshare resting against the wall of the half-open shed, one side of the house pockmarked with drying cowdung cakes.

What about the tribal woman, you might ask. Did she get home? Did she have a home? What about Chottu? Did he get home with the glittering Banarasi sari, the sari that was his payment, along with a few rupees, for letting in the murderers? Did he know Mrs Prasad's fate? Did he care about what happened to her in her home, that flat filled with the unused symbols of her children's absence, gadgets that she resented so much and that Chottu could only covet?

And what about the child who was buried by the roadside? Did he find his home there, under earth and rubble? Or will he be dug up one night by the foxes and dogs that have survived the monopoly of man? Will he be swept away during the next flood, washed into a tributary of the Ganges and from there into the Ganges and from there into the Bay of Bengal? Will the yet-unwalled waters of the oceans be his home?

There are things I cannot see in books.

And you may ask, where do homes begin? Do they begin out in the street, where the brick starts leading to the gate? Do they begin at the gate? Are they the village, the town, the city? Are they entire countries, and the keys to them stamped and signed passports, or are they just that small neighbourhood? Is home a brother, a sister, a mother, a father, a wife, a husband, a child; is home friends? Is home where you arrive or what you leave?

Or can a bus be home? There are conductors who sleep more in their buses than in their two-room houses with corrugated roofs on which a drizzle is like a waterfall. Ask Hari, he will tell you that he has spent more nights in his Ambassador taxi than with his wife. Ask Zeenat. Ask Wazir Mian: didn't he spend more years in various kitchens than he will ever spend in his sons' home?

Ask me, even me, for I have known houses all my life. Big, rooted homes, houses that once employed people like Wazir Mian, stole them from their homes, gave the gift of houses and resentment to their children. Ammi ké yahan and Ghar. I have carried these houses in my own way, on my own far more affluent shoulders. I have found and lost, lost and found my houses too. I make my home on buses and aeroplanes, in hotels and rented apartments. It was not an entirely free choice in my case either. I come from a place where choices are less free than they seem to be in some other places.

And in those other places, fingers are pointed. Look, say those who believe that they have deep-rooted homes, stop, stop, they exclaim as we pass their counters and gardens, look, look, look, they shout, for after centuries of eradicating the homeless, les marginaux, the landless peasantry, the gypsies, the wandering Jew, the bums, the lumpen proletariat, after centuries of planting people like trees, they still have us, and so they raise their fingers and shout, thief murderer stowaway immigrant.

I too know the dread of pointed fingers; I too can read what those distant lips frame.

Though sometimes things do take a turn, as the tabla master would have told you, laughing and coughing, coughing and laughing. Sometimes they do.